Once Upon A Time In Key West

A Brody Wahl Story

Wayne Gales

Copyright © 2026 Wayne Gales
All Rights Reserved
Written and Produced
by Wayne Gales
Conch Out Associates
Cover art by Tina Reigel
Edited by Peter Leonard
Contributor: Bill Black
Owner-operator
at Search and Salvage

Revised 2026

Dedicated to Russell Bricklin 'Bric' Wahl
You've lived rent-free in my head since I was a
boy.
I lived my life vicariously through you
for the past twelve years.
I'm a part of you as much as you
have been a part of me.

This novel is a work of fiction. Names, characters, places, and incidents are either the product of the author's imagination or, if real, used fictionally.

I'm just a nice guy with a few bad habits."
Bric Wahl

1
Close Only Counts In Horsehoes, Hand Grenades, and Most Thermonuclear Devices

Like many chapters in my father's life, this one started with a murder.

And almost ended with mine.

To make a long story short, I got hired by the Monroe County Sheriff's Office to help recover some victims of an apparent serial killer. Key West police and Monroe County Sheriff's had been working for weeks and getting nowhere, so the FDLE, Florida Department of Law Enforcement, sent an expert to see if any leads could be uncovered. Detective Charlotte Thomas didn't seem to be having any more luck than the locals, and bodies were popping up everywhere. Literally. Most of the bodies were found floating in the ocean near bridges; they were all fairly small, and most of them were registered sex offenders.

Or was it a coincidence?

What was worse, all of them had been found nude without a drop of blood in their body. They all had been mutilated, with their dick and balls either stuffed in their mouth or entirely missing, courtesy of the Florida Keys' active scavenger population that prowled every inch of the sea bottom constantly for tidbits. Toxicology reports from the autopsies showed the stomach contents in all of them were lousy with phenobarbital.

That little guy-sex offender/water burial pattern went away late one night when a larger body was found roadside instead of in Florida Bay. The investigation, which had become almost routine by now, stopped dead when I recognized the nude, mutilated body.

It was Monroe County Sheriff Jacob Sands. He was a good cop, my point of contact with Monroe County Sheriffs, and the guy who hired me. He had only mentioned a day earlier that he was zeroing in on a suspect or suspects. It was sad to see him go.

And I almost got fitted for wings the same night.

Since I lost my ride home from the crime scene up around mile 19 on US 1, Charlotte, a pretty FDLE detective, offered to take me home for a beverage.

Before we drove off, I could tell by her body language, a "come hither" smile, and an obvious display of various female body parts on the drive back into Key West told me we were heading to her place for more than a drink.

My little head was in charge of my big head. Again.

While we drove into town, Charly made some chit-chat while texting on her phone, a habit I don't admire when you're behind the wheel.

I expected we would be going to a hotel like La Concha, Pier House, Ocean Key, or the Reach, where Charly was staying while she was in Key West on assignment. I was surprised when she turned off Roosevelt Boulevard and pulled into the driveway of a large home in New Town not far behind the Publix Supermarket.

As we drove into the garage that Charly opened with the control clipped to her visor, she explained. "This house belongs to friends. They let me use it when I'm in town." With a little flirty giggle, she added, "More Conch relatives. Probably people we are both related to."

Charly closed the door behind us, noting, "You can't be too cautious these days. If I left the garage open all night, my car would be sitting on jacks by morning. I shouldn't give a fuck. After all, it's not even *my* car." With an authoritative voice, she declared, "Property of the State of Florida."

Charly motioned at the door, "There's a pool and hot tub in the backyard. Make yourself at home while I fix your drinks. You're welcome to take a dip or a soak. She paused and added, "You know, I think I'll join you for a drink; I've worked enough tonight." Holding my arms out, I answered, "I'd love to sit in the hot tub, but I don't have a bathing suit with me."

As she walked toward the house, turning slightly, she chuckled again, "Neither do I."

"I know how this night's gonna turn out," I thought to myself. I wandered out to the pool deck and considered shucking my clothes right there before Charly came out with the drinks, but I was just a little too modest to get naked in a stranger's backyard.

All in good time, Brody, my boy, all in good time.

I wandered around the yard for fifteen minutes before Charly came out with a tray and two oversized Solo Cups. Her blouse was unbuttoned to the waist. "The red cup is yours." She motioned, setting the drinks on a table. "I'm a bit of a lightweight, so mine is not as strong. I couldn't find anything to mix the rum with, so I took the liberty of making vodka and grapefruit if that's ok."

"Sure!" I said with a silly grin. I would drink Fireball if it meant I was going to get laid in a hot tub.

With a wink, she added. "I'll be back in a jiffy. I need to get out of these clothes. Meet you in the tub in two minutes!"

I picked up the red cup and took a big pull on the straw, wrinkling my nose at the taste of the bitter grapefruit juice. *"Oh well"*, I thought. I think my dad would agree: if a half-dressed woman offers you a drink, you drink. Holding the cup, I walked around the yard, not ready to undress yet. I saw a small shape emerge from the dark, and stiffened, in case it was an unfriendly dog. I was mildly surprised to see a potbellied pig, who came up to me and stretched his neck out, obviously looking for a treat. "Sorry, pig," I said, scratching him between the ears. "I doubt you like vodka." Other than a table, a couple of wooden Adirondack chairs, a cold firepit, and the pool with an attached hot tub, the yard looked featureless in the moonlight. Something caught my eye in the firepit, glinting in the moonlight. I stooped down and dug it out of the ashes.

It was a partially melted Sheriff's badge. I recognized the number as belonging to Jake Sands.

I looked down at the drink, and everything became clear in an instant. I tossed the rest of it against the wall. How much phenobarbital did I already have in me? Was just a sip enough to take me down? I almost didn't hear her come up behind me. I turned, and Charly was standing there, wearing just a black bra and thong bikini panties.

"I see you've met Man," she said with a laugh. "He's harmless, but he'll bug you endlessly for a treat." Noticing my empty cup she said with some concern, "Brody, you spilled your drink." She held her hand out for my cup. "Let me get you a refill…" Then she saw what was in my hand.

I squinted my eyes. Focus, Brody, focus.

There were two of her.

Charly spun around to run away. I reached for her shoulder, hoping I was grabbing at the right woman. All I caught was her bra strap. It came unhooked, but I held on to the strap. She spun around, facing me, standing in a way that told me she had been trained in hand-to-hand fighting. All those tedious days with my wife Mallory in my living room took over. Mallory's number one rule said, "If you're going to fight, fight dirty." Without a windup, I kicked Charly in the crotch as hard as I could and followed up with a hard clip to the jaw, almost falling down in the process. She collapsed in a heap. I tried to catch her to keep her from falling in the hot tub where she would have drowned for sure but missed, and she fell in, head first, with a loud splash. By now I was barely able to stand. I dug in my pocket for my phone and punched 911, and I was down on my hands and knees by the time the phone answered.

"911, what's your emergency?" I tried to focus enough to give her an answer.

"This is Brody Wahl. I'm doing some work for the Monroe County Sheriff's. I think I know who the serial killer is. Call my uncle, Officer John Russell, and let him know." Words were starting to slur. "Send some cops over here right now!" Looking at the lifeless body floating in the tub, I added, "And send an ambulance! Hurry."

Despite my voice, the operator didn't sound rushed or impressed. "Mister ah, Wahl, since you're calling from a cell phone and we can only approximate your location. What is your address?"

"Fuck lady, I don't know!" I wracked my brain for a moment. "Ah, we turned right off Linda and went a few houses down the street. Don't know the address!" I was lying flat on my back now, and the whole world was spinning like a top. I remembered two more details. "It's a white house, I think, with a two-car garage." I dropped the phone beside me and rolled over. The last thing I saw before passing out was a skinny naked woman with flabby tits holding a big knife walking around the pool toward me.

If it's any consolation, I was blissfully unconscious and didn't feel the six stab wounds that went into my back and legs.

2
Sleep Is Overrated

My father told me about this once from first-hand experience, but I didn't pay attention at the time. Now I understand what he was telling me. "When you sleep, you almost always dream. You might remember the dream, or most often, the memory vanishes the moment you wake up. It's like grabbing a cloud of smoke that's just out of reach, and there's a sense of time passing. You might not know if it's been two hours or ten, but you definitely know you have been sleeping for some period." What he said next I remember vividly now. "But when you have been sedated, there's no passage of time, no dreaming, nothing. You die a little, I think."

When I woke up, it took a few minutes before I became aware of my surroundings. I could hear quiet voices, felt pain, and saw blurry shapes, but nothing else. After a minute or two, I realized I was lying on my stomach, looking through a hole in a special hospital bed, at a featureless white tiled floor. Suddenly my memory started coming back.

Bad cop, hot tub, badge, drugged drink, knife.

Oh shit, my dick!

I tried to reach under my body to check for my frank and beans, but with IVs in both arms and my hands strapped to the side of the bed to keep from jerking them out of my arms, I couldn't do much more than scratch my hips.

"Relax, buckaroo, it's all there. Somehow she missed the family jewels, but she scored just about everywhere else on your body."

Even though I couldn't see him, the unmistakable growl of my father's gravely voice filled the recovery room. "She did manage to nick a kidney, slice off the tip of your liver and collapse a lung," he added, "but nothing important."

"You might call those body parts unimportant," I said, through clenched teeth, "but I've grown rather fond of them."

"You might have a point there, son, you just might have a point," he answered.

When I got moved into a regular room and got to lie painfully on my side, my father was there every day from the time they let him in in the morning until they kicked him out when visiting hours were over; he parked in the chair next to my bed except for the times a nurse or doctor had to commit some indiscretion to my body. Bric was in his mid-seventies, a little less spry, but always with that twinkle in his eye, as if he knew something you didn't. He'd walk past the nurse's station every day like he owned the place, as close to the beginning of visitors' hours (or before), wearing cargo shorts, Reef sandals, Costa prescription sunglasses, and a long-billed Coastal Angler fishing cap. Every morning he always asked if he could get me anything. *Yeah, Dad, a double cheese Whopper, hold the pickles, lettuce, and tomatoes, large fry, and a Big Gulp. Why do you ask if you know they won't let you sneak it in?* He also kept me abreast of developments.

"That bitch that stabbed you owned the house where Charly was staying, apparently in a lesbian relationship," Bric said, shaking his head. "She flew the coop before the cops found you and hasn't been seen since. Lillian Albury, no doubt a distant conch relative." Noting the obvious, Dad added, "This rock ain't that big. She either fled up the Keys that night or is doing a damn good job of hiding. All they know was she had an old green Hyundai with Florida plates," he added with a smile. "And you know, she used to work in this very hospital as a nurse? That's where all the phenobarbital was coming from, and the big bowl of oxycodone they found on the kitchen table." Bric chuckled. "Would you believe that Vietnamese Pot-Bellied pig that lived there with them is an addict? They must have been giving him drugs on demand every day. I hear he's driving the gang at animal control nuts with his constant squealing. I suspect soon somebody is either going to slip him a pill or put a bullet in him."

3
Rum and Chocolate Ice Cream

Being cooped up in a hospital for a month might sound like a good time if you're eighty-five years old and the highlight of your day is a sponge bath with an eighteen-year-old candy striper graced with overdeveloped secondary sexual characteristics. Come to think of it, that part doesn't sound too bad if the Lower Keys Medical Center employed such a creature, but my semi-regular duty nurse was, as my dad would say, a bit over-nourished, a bit over the hill, and beyond homely. Oh, I'm not knocking the profession. A professional hospital nurse is underpaid, has skills beyond her training, will attend to you a dozen times a day, clean up after your messes, and wipe your bottom when you potty. They should wear a cape and have a big 'S' emblazoned on their chest.

Only THIS chest had room to write *"Superman, don't tug on my cape unless it's a life-threatening emergency."*

My nurse, call her Hilda, had to take on double duty when my physician popped in maybe every other day. Looking at my chart, he'd ask, "How are we doing today?", all the while backing out of my room before he could get an answer. I shouldn't complain. He patched me up, inside and out, and held off the grim reaper for at least a few more laps around the sun. Doctor Lewis is the same dude that stitched up my dad when Itchy Roberts shoved that saber through him at Fantasy Fest all those years ago. Lewis was an eager new resident at the hospital back then. Now he's an old salt, and a few puncture wounds in a healthy young man hardly give him more than a casual nod, a few *dozen or fifty* stitches, and prescribed bed rest for a lengthy period. When I'm sprung from this jail, no doubt there will be dozens of follow-up appointments every two weeks, as long as insurance would pay. And I anticipated a buttload of physical therapy.

I'd rather be diving.

Ah, insurance. Actually, I didn't have any other than my DAN (Divers Alert Network) insurance. I didn't think I would ever do anything really dangerous again when I wasn't underwater.

Boy did I get that part wrong.

Actually, Monroe County grudgingly admitted that I was technically on my way home from an assignment and in the company of a state officer when my "accident" happened, even though I was not a real employee but a contract worker.

The little detail that the State Officer tried to kill me was just an overlooked technicality.

Don't bother joining my pity party, or feeling bad for poor old Broderick Wahl, all cooped up alone in a hospital room for three weeks. Truth is, between Nurse Hilda, housekeeping, the janitor (*sorry, Custodial Services),* and the night nurse that delighted in rousing me every two hours throughout the night to take my temperature, blood pressure, and give me a laxative even though they have pumped enough meds into me that I'm so constipated that I may never shit again, and something to help me sleep- "*Wake up Broderick! It's time for your sleeping medication"*, I was never alone.

With an estimate that I might not get sprung from this place for a few weeks, then bed rest for a month after, I had a problem that I needed to deal with in a hurry.

My father, one Russell Bricklin 'Bric' Wahl.

After years of high-risk living and a disregard for a healthy diet, *like I should talk*, Bric's love of rum and chocolate ice cream had finally given him a diagnosis of type two diabetes, and get this, he has to get a testosterone shot every two weeks. His libido hasn't left, but his, ah, performance has started to show a shortcoming or two. I had to start giving him shots to keep him from throwing himself off the roof of the La Concha. Top that off with a daily M&M's bag full of meds, and my ne'er-do-well father had become high maintenance. If I didn't hand him his daily dose, and stick him myself, it would probably never happen.

Anyway, with me out of commission, there was nobody to perform these duties. Karen? She was long gone, living in anonymity on some ranch in Oklahoma. I feared that ship had sailed. Oh, she might come if I asked, but frankly, I had no idea how to even reach her.

I wracked my brain and finally came up with a solution. Maybe the only solution. My half-sister Mary Beth. I called the local news rag, The Key West Citizen, as soon as I thought of her. She knew I was in the hospital; heck, everyone south of Key Largo knew.

The story, minus the gruesome details, was splashed all over the front page for three days in a row. "SERIAL MURDER CASE SOLVED! LOCAL DIVER NARROWLY ESCAPES DEATH!" When I reached Mary, she began apologizing profusely for not having visited. "I didn't know if you were out of the ICU. I'll come over right now".

I was kind of hoping she would come and go before

Dad showed up so I could ease into the conversation a bit at a time. She still wasn't warm and fuzzy with Dad, but the last few times we had all been together, at least she didn't have her hands around his throat. My plan went all to hell when Bric sauntered in an hour early, with a trail of yelling nurses in his wake.

He had hardly sat down in the chair when the click of heels announced my sister had arrived. She started to reach toward me for a hug when she froze in her tracks at the sight of my father next to the bed. A King Cobra would have received a warmer welcome.

"What the hell is he doing here?" She almost spat the words out.

"Well, he IS my father, and for that matter, he's also yours."

She turned to storm out of the room and only hesitated when I cried, "Wait!" Rising up on one elbow, and wincing from the stitches in my back, I barely got out the words. "I asked you to come for a reason. I need a favor, a HUGE favor." I went on to explain that for at least the next few weeks, somebody had to take care of Dad and make sure he got his daily meds and shots.

"The *Seaglass* has lots of space. You would have a private master bedroom, a live-in cook, and we're docked on Stock Island. Mary, he needs this. If he doesn't get his shots and take his meds, it could kill him." I finished with my best lost-puppy look. Bric responded, almost snarling at me. "I can take care of myself." But I could see his shoulders slump a little. He raised the only person more stubborn than he.

"Isn't there someone else?" Mary Beth bit off the words. "How about your friend Kevin? Couldn't he do this for you?"

Kevin Montclaire, owner and manager at *Hunks*, a bar on Duval that Dad once built and owned, was a six-foot-five, three-hundred-pound drag queen named Scarlett working at Aqua when I was a boy, and one of the nicest, kindest people I have ever met.

Bric shook his head. For once he didn't seem to have much fight in him. "Kevin would take a bullet for me, and for that matter, I would for him, but he can't handle even the sight of a needle. One look and he would faint dead away before the syringe came out of the bottle."

I could see Mary Beth was starting to understand my predicament. She looked at my father with her hands on her hips. "Bric, to be honest, I wouldn't piss on you if you were on fire." She stood for a minute, seemed to consider something, and came to a decision.

Pointing at me, she said, "Brody, you're my brother. I will do this for *you*, not for *him*." Acting as if he wasn't in the room she turned again to walk out and said over her shoulder, "Text me the address. I'll be there tonight." I thought she was going to storm out, but she put her purse on the table and sat down in a chair.

Dad, being the sarcastic asshole he could be, stood up, acted as if Mary Beth wasn't in the room, and slapped me on the knee, the only body part at the moment that wasn't bandaged or subject to pain.

"Well, that went well." Mary Beth almost got up and left, realized the joke was on her, and even managed a little smile.

"When you get better, Brody, I've got an opportunity for us to work on." He held up a hand, knowing the son was about to lecture the father. "Not like I'll be getting wet. That duty will be yours once you're back in shape." That perked me up. "What kind of project?"

"I got a call that a boat out of Sebastian needs an experienced diver with good breath. There's as much free diving as scuba from what I hear. I seem to recall," he said with a sly smile, "that you can hold your breath longer than most."

"Sebastian?" I answered with a frown. "Other than that little sand bar in the middle of a protected area by Sebastian inlet that we both know about and don't dare return to, almost every square yard of sand between Fort Pierce and Melbourne with a decent mag hit has been picked nearly clean." I thought for a moment and added, "Not like there might be the occasional find, but I think most of the good stuff has been salvaged.

"And that's just it," he answered. "This boat won't be dragging electronics too much. The skipper has some leads on some other places in the area that have never been worked. I think it just might be an angle that could pay off. Remember, there are still four or five ships from the 1715 fleet that have never been found." Holding his arms wide and issuing his all too familiar statement, "It's a big ocean. They *are* out there somewhere."

Treasure hunting and shipwreck salvaging is a gift, or a curse, depending on how you look at it, that goes back many generations on both sides of my family tree. The hint that someone may have a line on the half-billion dollars' worth of silver, emeralds, and gold that is still lying somewhere off the Florida east coast made me try to raise up on one elbow again. Pain shot up my arm, through my neck, and down my back. I lay back down in a hurry. Through gritted teeth, I croaked, "What's the name of the skipper and the boat?"

Still smiling a little, Bric sounded a little cagy. "The captain, you'll meet in due time. The boat," Dad consulted an email on his phone, "is the *Hoedown*."

Dad got up to leave and tried to give Mary Beth a hug, but she shied away like he was on fire. "Not so fast, Bric," Mary said with a warning tone. "I'll be your caregiver for a few months, but it's not like we've become lifelong chums. Yet."

Dad tipped his cap and bowed in semi-mock respect. "Yes, ma'am. Got it, ma'am."

I could see she was tempted to deck him right there with a roundhouse swing, then thought better of it.

He turned to me before he walked out. "Brody, could you tell Mary where the new injector needles are hidden? I managed to stick myself last night, and the needle was so dull you would have thought I was shoving a ten-penny nail in my ass."

I laughed. That hurt too.

Gotta love him.

4
Go To Hell And Wait

It seemed like forever, but it was only three weeks before I was a free man. Mary had a bed set up for me in the lounge so I didn't have to navigate the stairs. Much to my surprise and pleasure, Mary Beth still hung around even after I was able to administer nightly doses to my father's hairy ass. She even brought a boyfriend over one night and cooked dinner. I'm pretty sure I heard her boy toy sneak off the boat at five the next morning.

I'm also sure he didn't stay over just for milk and cookies.

Bric and Mary even seemed to be getting along. At least after six weeks, there were no visible scars on my dad, and that's good enough for me.

My recovery progressed steadily, from being able to use my left hand and eat without assistance to climbing stairs and even occasionally venturing into town for dinner. At least once every few weeks, we all took the flats boat out for some quiet time near Marvin Key, munching on Key West pink shrimp while waist-deep in crystal-clear water that was as warm as a bathtub. It reminded me of stories Bric told me so many times with our late friend Rumpy and gave me the chance to absorb my two most important vitamins: Vitamin D and Vitamin Sea.

Part of my recovery regimen was a habit I got into when I was getting in shape with Mallory. It was something I hated more than a root canal but knew it was a necessary evil. I started jogging again.

At first, it was just around the marina where Seaglass was docked, jogging more slowly than a ninety-year-old man using a walker. As soon as I could make a few laps around the marina without heaving my guts out, I graduated off Stock Island and to the Key West Airport and back.

Finally, after a month or so, I set out for Old Town. Instead of keeping to the busy streets, I varied my route every day, peeling off Truman over to the cemetery, *where I'm related to about a third of the residents*, then down little side streets like Poor House Lane, Petronius, Whitman, and Angela, jogging past hundred-year-old houses, old carriage barns, countless un-trimmed trees, and overgrown gardens. Some houses were beautifully maintained or carefully restored, and some were literally falling down in a tragic heap of termite-ridden scrap wood.

There were exotic smells of flowers, combined with the smell of cooking bacon and the occasional whiff of someone's cannabis habit. Besides the smell of dope, the scenery made the run at least tolerable. It took almost six months before I started to return to some semblance of normal.

One afternoon, Dad brought up a subject he had mentioned when I was in the hospital.

"Brody, remember when I told you I had heard about a boat that needed a duck foot or two named the *Hoedown*? From what I remember, it's getting close to the time of year that people on the east coast of Florida usually start treasure hunting in earnest."

"Who is the skipper?" I asked, "Have I ever met him?"

Bric got that twinkle back in his eye for a moment. It made me feel good to see that, even for a moment. Instead of answering my question, he got that faraway look.

"That's right", Bric repeated, almost nostalgically, "It's about the time of year, from June to October, when the wind shifts from the east and comes mostly from the west, making the water fairly calm, except," he said with a smile, "for when there's rain with a name in the area, and diving for treasure off the Florida coast is possible, or at least more convenient". He closed his eyes with fond memories.

"Ah, the *Hoedown*. Fine treasure boat from what I remember. Nice cabin with lots of shade, a galley so you can eat more than three-day-old Publix chicken for lunch, and electrically operated twin mailboxes on the stern." With a smile, he added, "You met the skipper a long time ago, but I would be surprised if you will recall. Remember back when you were a pimple-faced teenager, I used to sit in occasionally with the *Waiters* when they were short a bass player?"

"Yeah, I sort of remember. Wasn't the band run by a lady? Helen something." I was curious now. "Which band member is running a boat now?"

His twinkle turned into a wider grin. Still ignoring my question, he answered, "That's the group. Helen O'Rourke. She called herself Helen Waite. The band was *Helen Waite and the Waiters.*" I could see my father reminiscing, almost to the point a little tear appeared. "They played all over. Sloppy Joes, Hogs Breath, Captain Tony's. Anytime someone complained about the music choices, or how long we took breaks, or if we were late to a gig, and asked us who to talk to, we just told them to go to hell and wait."

He was almost laughing now.

"Funny story," I agreed, a little sarcastically, "but what does this have to do with a dive boat in Sebastian, old man?"

Bric held up his hands in a "stop" motion. "Hold your horses, son. I'm getting there. Don't interrupt a good story."

Bric went to the little wet bar in the lounge, poured himself a rum drink, and sat down on the couch. I wasn't sure that alcohol was a prudent additive to all those prescriptions he has to take every morning, but it wasn't my business to give counsel. After a few long pulls on the boat drink, he realized I was still standing there, waiting for him to continue.

"Oh, back to the *Hoedown*," he said, swirling the ice cubes in his now empty solo cup. He held the cup toward me for a refill. I complied as quickly as possible, keeping my back to my dad so he couldn't see I poured a lighter portion of rum. Handing it back, he thanked me with a nod, took another sip, and curled his nose. "I've drunk wine coolers that were stronger than this." Regardless, he took another drink. After a few minutes, I got impatient.

"Dad, the boat?" I implored. *"Focus, Bric, focus"*, I thought, impatiently

"Oh yeah, where were we? Ah, the *Hoedown*. Anyway, Helen's husband ran a salvage boat up in Marathon for years, finding a few silver cobs here and there, but not much more, just enough to keep him going. One day they found the *Hoedown*, hard up on a reef, with Henry nowhere in sight. The Coast Guard searched for days before they found him, lying on the bottom of Hawk Channel. He must have been by himself, and either had a heart attack or stroke.

Helen had often gone out with her husband to become a pretty savvy skipper. She folded the band, moved to Sebastian, and has been running a little salvage operation ever since, never with any big finds, but enough to keep fuel in the boat and food on the table."

"And you said she's on to something?" I asked eagerly. "She found one of the missing ships?"

Dad fielded that question cautiously. "A real treasure hunter will share breakfast, dinner, liquor, spare pocket money, or extra engine parts with you without blinking an eye," Bric said. "But share what they know about the whereabouts of silver or gold?"

With a little chuckle, he noted as seriously as possible, "You might as well piss into the wind. I told you in the hospital that a friend of a friend told me about the *Hoedown*. They knew Helen and I worked together in the past, and that she was looking for a crew, a *good* crew. It just seems she's putting extra effort into stocking up with supplies and prep like she's maybe on to something. Nothing set in stone, but I have been given the impression she has come up with a clue or an angle." Bric stabbed me in the chest with a finger. "Either way, Brody, I think it's a good idea you at least pay a visit."

Something occurred to me. "Hey, you and Helen must be about the same age, give or take a few. Did you ever, ah…..."

Dad's response was almost a growl. "Henry was a friend, a *good* friend. Even *I* have boundaries, sort of, most of the time. Not that Helen isn't a looker, but she was about as married a person as I'd ever met, and after Henry died, she blew out of the Keys before I ever turned my radar on, and", he added with a little smile. "Besides, I couldn't find where she went for years, not that I didn't look for her."

"If I'm up there for the summer, who's gonna stick your butt every night?", I asked. Dad stiffened up a little. "I can take care of myself. Don't let me get in the way of your adventures." I sat there with my arms folded and looked stubborn. He realized I wasn't ready to be away from him.

"Listen, if it makes you any happier, you can ask your sister Mary Beth to babysit again. I'm sure you can sweet talk her into playing nurse on a yacht again for a few months."

I half expected my sister to firmly turn down my offer, which would have been fine with me. I'd really rather spend time with my father. After all, he's no spring chicken, and he seemed to be losing weight, but a deal's a deal, and Mary Beth agreed to assume nurse duties again with little hesitation, this time for the whole summer. She agreed, provided that we let her boyfriend stay with her on Seaglass. I should say fiancée, as her left hand sported a ring.

I didn't ask, and she didn't say. Dad didn't mention the ring, but I have no doubt he saw it. Bric doesn't miss much.

"It's no biggie if her dude wants to hang out on the boat at night," Bric agreed, "*Seaglass* can sleep ten. Three, make that four with the cook, still leaves plenty of space to rattle around in." Dad brightened a little. "I hope he's good at chess. I'm getting tired of kicking Mary Beth's ass in a dozen moves even when I spot her a knight."

I understood that. I've never beaten my dad at chess since he taught me at age eight. Not once.

5
Hoedown

Two weeks later, my father and I found ourselves sitting on the Hoedown, firmly tied up at a marina near Sebastian, Florida. We took my Jeep since Dad's clunker Toyota wasn't reliable enough to go to Hogfish Bar and Grille for lunch, much less make a round trip to Sebastian- especially after Mr. Goodman's pilot, Billy, plugged it full of holes when he took care of the guys that had kidnapped my father.

My Wrangler isn't much to look at. The doors and canvas top are permanently stored in the rafters at the garage behind *Hunks*. With a faded paint job and rusty black wheels, she looked like somebody's beater and wasn't a candidate for car theft, and that's the look I was aiming for. The outside may have been, er, rustic, but I kept everything under the hood in tip-top condition, with an overbuilt, turbo-driven V8, a heavy-duty Dana transfer case, and a Dana Spicer JK Ultimate Dana 60 Axle Assembly. It's a sweet ride for sure.

Dad climbed into the right seat, graced with an old beach towel so the springs didn't poke up and bite your ass, and looked at me with a little disgust. I had to laugh inwardly, thinking of the Volkswagen Thing that his girlfriend Karen Murphy sold him years ago. It was mostly rusted where the fenders used to be, and Dad had to pop-rivet a cookie sheet to the passenger-side floor to keep any rider from playing Fred Flintstone down Duval Street.

"What happens if it starts raining?" Bric asked,

looking at the sky.

"Duh, we get wet." That stopped the questions. He took one last accusing glance at the sky, folded his arms, and responded with a disgusted, "Hrump".

Back to the *Hoedown*.

Like most working boats, there weren't a lot of chairs to sit on. Actually, there weren't *any* chairs to sit on. Bric found an ice chest to park on, I sat on a milk crate and Helen sat on the rail by the mailboxes. I instantly liked her. Soft-spoken, attractive, a little plus-sized but in the places that counted, and I could tell by her presence, as tough as nails. I was a little surprised by how much younger she appeared than I assumed, since I figured Dad played in her band almost twenty years ago. She couldn't be much more than her late forties, maybe early fifties, not *that* much older than me.

Hmmm….

"Stop thinking with the little head, Brody", I thought. *"The last time you did that, you almost lost the little head, along with other precious body parts."*

And my life.

I straightened up a little, focused on the conversation, and made a mental note to keep this strictly business. Helen was talking about the area's history, a subject Dad and I were more than familiar with, but we let her tell us her version. After all, it's good to hear it from an experienced local. You always learn something. I paused and asked a sort of rhetorical, but pointed, question. *Mallory, my ex, taught me that word too.*

"So, boats drag a magnetometer through the water to find ferrous metal 'hits', assuming that non-ferrous material, like silver, gold, and emeralds from a wreck, are nearby." I made the point with my finger. "Hasn't this water been literally magged and blown to death over the years?"

Helen lapsed into a well-rehearsed speech, much like my father does when he's educating people, who often don't need the education.

"The magnetometer is connected to a laptop with a program on it like a regular oscilloscope, let's say with a baseline reading of 50,000 gamma. You tune that baseline to the center of the scope. If you run over a cannon, an anchor, or the abandoned block from a fifty-seven Chevy, the signal jumps off the screen.

Also, the strength of the hit is relative to the distance from the towed array, so there is a good bit of interpretation in the process." With a bit of a sad smile, she added, "Of course, most of the easy-to-find cannon and anchors are long gone, pulled up decades ago and sold to adorn gas stations, souvenir shops, or some rich guy's front lawn."

"So, you look for something smaller?" I asked.

"Right," she answered, a little sarcastically. "In shallow water, if you run over a musket, the scope will jump fifteen or twenty Tesla. That's the term we use now. And a nail or spike will indicate no more than a 'one' or 'two'. Normally, the scope will drift up and down without any material to 'hit' on, but it will hardly move at all if you go over a wreck site without any big ferrous metal.

"Can't you just rig something that will find non-ferrous metal?" I asked. "I've used several that detect gold and silver up to ten inches. A good Aquapulse or Pulse 8X will find a beer can bottom at three feet or a coin at eighteen inches. Couldn't you just scale that up to something that you could tow behind a boat?"

She gave that smile again as if she was explaining to someone that the world wasn't flat, the tooth fairy was mom or dad, and that Santa Claus couldn't visit every house in the world in one night without exceeding the speed of light.

"Oh, you could, I suppose, but you would need a platform about as big as a movie theater screen and a power supply that only a nuclear sub could create."

It was Dad's turn to smile. "I know some peeps in the CIA," he offered. "Maybe we could borrow a boomer for a weekend."

"There would be a little side effect to something that powerful," Helen pointed out. "You would barbecue every dolphin, lobster, snapper, or shark you passed over while it was transmitting. There would be a path of crispy critters behind you." She leaned forward a little. "That just might get a little attention from Greenpeace, Fish & Game, and every little granny from Miami to Daytona Beach, but at the same time you could open a great discount fried seafood stand on US 1..."

I nodded my head. "Okay, bad idea. So, if almost all of the guns and anchors are gone, and you almost can't identify any other wrecks, and anyway, if all the good spots have already been blown and searched, how do you find any good stuff?"

Helen got up and went into the cabin, emerging with a clipboard holding two printed Excel sheets. I could see a bunch of GPS coordinates on the sheets as she walked back to her perch. Holding up the clipboard, she pointed to the lines. "We don't

Mag much at all. There are enough locations on this sheet to last us a year or three."

"And where, may I ask, did you get those numbers?" Dad cracked. "What do you know that other people don't?"

I've seen that Cheshire Cat smile before, the same one on Alice in Alice in Wonderland. And occasionally, on my father as well.

"That's for me to know, period. I'll put you over one of these spots, you go down and find something for us to look at, I position *Hoedown* over the spot, dust off the overburden with the mailboxes, then you go back down and see what you can find." With a furrowed brow, she added. "These are hunches, but good hunches. I think I might be onto something."

We stood to leave, and I could tell Helen had something else to say.

"I need to ask, Brody; divers I hire always ask me about pay, benefits, housing, things like that. You haven't asked a single question about that. Why?"

I could see Dad looking away, taking an intense interest in a lone pelican sitting on a piling a few hundred yards away. I could tell this answer was mine to field.

"Well, Mrs. O'Rourke, ah, Ms. Wait." I hesitated, and looked her in the eyes "Ma'am I actually don't know how you want to be called."

"Well, Ma'am isn't one of them. My name is Helen, plain and simple, but people around her mostly call me Cap." With her hands on her hips, she explained, "Brody, this will be a summer of lousy food, lousy pay, lousy accommodations, and when you're not in the water, an environment hotter than a pizza oven.

You might work twenty-one days in a row if we find something worth working, and you might sit on your ass and play poker that long or longer if the wind blows the wrong way or a storm is nearby. I won't promise you'll bring up more than a few ballast stones and a piece of broken pottery all summer."

Then she smiled. "But if, and it's a mighty 'iffy' if, we find a previously unfound wreck from the 1715 fleet, we all get a share of the booty. I'm sure you know of divers that have hit it big." Helen swept an arm toward the Atlantic in a wide gesture, much like my dad does. "There's a buttload of silver and gold out there, somewhere. It's our goal to find some of it." She looked soft for a moment. "Did I scare you off?"

"Actually, I do know people that have scored big," I thought. *"Firsthand, but nothing we need to share with her."*

"Cap, I'm not in this for the money." I explained, "If we do score, that's a bonus, but it's the adventure, and it's the chance that I can put my hands on gold or silver that hasn't been touched for over three hundred years. *That's* my motivation." I held out a hand. "Cap, you've got yourself a diver."

Before leaving, she left us with one last thought. "As your skipper, especially as one of the only women treasure dive boat captains in the area, I have a few rules for you to keep in mind." She held up a finger, "One, no drinking onboard or within 24 hours of getting wet. Two. No drugs, of any kind. Zero. Zip. Nada on board or on shore. If I catch you or find out you've been using, you're out. Three. If I hear you curse, you better have dropped a gold bar on your big toe. Four. No cheating. Don't hide something of value on or in a body part, or on the bottom to 'find' later when you happen to be 'spearfishing' in the same area." Helen gave a kind smile. "Sorry, Brody, but I have to be half Glenda the good witch and the other half Darth Vader. Those are my version of The Cider House Rules." She pointed to the doorway leading into the cabin. "They will be posted there before day one. Simple, firm, and non-negotiable." She looked at me with a questioning look. "Scare you off yet?

"No, ma'am," I answered, "I don't do drugs, I never curse, and I never steal. As for liquor, it will do me good to have a dry summer."

6
|Flashback
Somewhere east of present-day Sebastian, Florida, August 1, 1715

The *General Antonio de Echeverz* lay fourteen miles off the east coast of *La Florida* in one hundred feet of water. Her three masts, torn off and in tatters, left her more or less intact but damaged to the point she would never sail again. The *Echeverz* was not a large ship, slightly over 120 feet long and 45 feet wide. Built to travel with ships much better armed, she only sported twenty-four guns.

Her rowboat had vanished overboard in the hurricane that had devastated the combined vessels of two Spanish treasure fleets returning from the New World to Spain. The combined group, *Nueva España Fleet*, under Capt.-General Don Juan Esteban de Ubilla, and the *Tierra Firme Fleet*, under Don Antonio de Echeverz y Zubiza, had sailed from Havana, Cuba.

At two in the morning on Wednesday, July 31, 1715, all eleven ships of the fleet were lost in a hurricane along the East coast of Florida. A 12th ship, the French frigate "*Le Grifon*", had sailed with the fleet. Its Captain was unfamiliar with the Florida coastline and elected to stay further out to sea.

The "*Grifon*" safely returned to Europe. With the coast over the horizon of the *Echeverz*, especially with the crow's nest lying in the water beside the ship, the captain and crew were unaware the ten other ships had wrecked in the storm, and nearly fifteen hundred of their fellow sailors had perished. Most of the other ships lay foundered on the beach, or sunk near the shoreline, out of sight of the crew. Not even knowing how far from the distant shore they were, the sailors had little thought of even trying to strike for the shore.

They were also aware that the coastal waters were heavily patrolled by bull, tiger, and hammerhead sharks, as well as the occasional great white shark. Since most of them could not swim, the only chance would be by clinging onto loose wood, and the predators made that option improbable if not impossible. Shortly after daylight, the ship's carpenters wasted no time tearing planks off the deck and rails to fashion a makeshift boat so they could row to shore.

General Antonio de Echeverz had picked up precious freight in South America before sailing with mostly silver 'cobs', two-, four-, and eight-real silver coins, and several gold bars. The ship was also loaded with precious porcelain and silks, transported painfully from China to the West Coast of Mexico, transported by mule to Valparaíso on the East Coast, and then to Havana by ship, where it was loaded on the *Echeverz* as it joined the remaining ships to Spain

The other group, led by Capt. Gen. Juan Esteban de Ubilla, loaded up with more treasure from Mexico. The primary cargo on all the ships was silver, which is why the combined convoy is often referred to as the *Flota de la Plata*, or Plate Fleet. Plata means silver in Spanish. But there was plenty of gold, too, and vanilla, chocolate, sassafras, and other sumptuous luxuries for the folks back home. Like all galleons leaving *Nuevo España*, there was almost as much undocumented cargo aboard as freight on the official manifest.

Personal hordes of china, silks, and spices were counted among items not listed, and more than a little gold and silver, and at least one special cargo, had been carefully hidden by officers, clergy, and officials. The value of the unlisted items could amount to millions of escudos.

Sitting in 100 feet of water, *General Antonio de Echeverz* sat at anchor against the edge of the Gulfstream current. With the seas calm as glass after the storm, sailors felt confident enough to build a fire in a large sandbox in the middle of the main deck, where they prepared a stew and dried their wet clothes. Sailors were always fearful of fire on the wooden ships, and great care was always taken to keep the flames away from wood, but the crew didn't notice the deck had separated slightly in the storm, allowing a few coals to slip between the cracks.

Directly below lay a store of black powder, stored in wooden kegs and arranged in the middle of the lower deck to be available near her cannon in case of an attack by pirates or marauding English ships. When the coals touched the powder, the result was immediate, spectacular, and devastating.

The ship blew up with a tremendous explosion, throwing her four-thousand-pound guns into the water like so many toothpicks. The hull blew apart, and the valuables immediately followed the ballast stones straight to the bottom. The disaster killed half the sailors instantly, and those that survived the blast were thrown into the Atlantic. Unable to swim, they either drowned in a few moments or, clinging to floating debris, faced the hungry mouths of the ever-present pelagic predators long before they could reach the distant coastline.

There were no survivors. The explosion was heard by the sailors from the other wrecks that had dragged themselves to shore. The wet and bedraggled sailors huddled on the beach heard the explosion, never knowing what had caused it.

7
Booger

We ran back down the Keys to drop Dad off, and he watched with an amused look while I loaded up the Jeep with my dive gear. Despite big shocks and a two-inch lift kit, the little Wrangler literally groaned under the weight.

"What are you gonna salvage, the Titanic?" Dad observed. "Trust me from experience. You need a mask, fins, a snorkel, a regulator, a weight belt, and a couple of spare T-shirts. You can leave the rest of this hoard on the *Seaglass*."

Boy, did he get that part right.

I have to admit, I've been a little spoiled, diving off the *Never on Saturday*, a yacht-turned salvage boat by my ex-wife's grandparents, Moishe and Golda Cohen, and our own *Seaglass*, a hundred-and-fifty-five-foot motorsailer, given to my father and me from Mallory's late godfather. Mr. Goodman was an old man with fabulous wealth and a meticulous desire to not let you know where it came from. The *Hoedown* and the diving company around it was a little more spartan. Actually, it was a lot more spartan.

Not knowing what to expect when I got to Sebastian, I followed Helen to a house in Wabasso. A kindly old woman named Becky answered the door and walked us down a hall to a ten-foot-square room with two bunk beds. "I make breakfast every morning at six," Becky said with a kindly, but no bullshit voice. "If you get up at six-thirty, you drive through Duncan Donuts."

"Four people in one little room?" I asked. "Isn't that a little cramped?"

Becky pointed down the hall. "There's a storeroom down the hall for your gear and extra clothes. Housing is almost impossible in this neck of the woods." She narrowed her eyes. "You're welcome to sleep in your Jeep unless you're wealthy enough to rent a three-bedroom condo."

The thought of my own place crossed my mind, but the rest of the crew would never respect a snooty rich kid.

"Oh, this will do just fine," I answered. "I'm sure I'll be too tired at night to do much more than sleep." I scanned the room. The two lower bunks had clothes piled on them, making it clear that one of the empty top bunks would be my home. *That's fine*, I thought to myself; at least I won't be drunk on a Saturday night, fall out of the bunk, *and break my neck*.

I pointed to the other beds. "Who are my roommates?"

"One guy that's on a different boat than you," Helen answered. "I don't remember his name, but the other one is from Key West, like you. He'll be your dive partner on the *Hoedown*. You might know him; he's about your age. He dived for me last year, and I brought him back."

I perked up when I heard it was someone from the rock. "Who?" I asked.

"Fredrick Russell Thomas," Helen answered. "We all call him Freddie."

"Booger Thomas?" I asked, with a little disgust. "He couldn't find a turd in a kiddie pool."

Helen remarked with a concerned look. "Do you

have a problem with Freddie? Dive partners have to get along, in and out of the water. Something I need to know?"

"Booger and I had more than one run-in when we were in high school," I answered. "That was a long time ago." With a little sigh, not wanting to worry Helen, I added. "If he's willing to let bygones be bygones, I'm good to forget the past."

They say a leopard never changes its spots, nor a skunk its stripes.

"Why do you call him Booger?" Helen asked.

"Because through most of high school, he kept one finger in his nose, picking it, and his head up his ass," I answered with a sniff.

We heard a noise from the front of the house and a clump down the hall.

Staring at the figure entering the room, I added, "And he's my second cousin."

"Well, as I live and breathe! If it ain't Brody the Toady!"

I folded my arms and counted to five chimpanzees, but couldn't help using his old nickname,

"Hey, Booger, what's new?"

He took a step toward me. "My name's Fred, Freddie to my friends. You can call me Mister Thomas."

"In your dreams," was all I cared to answer.

"Boys. BOYS!" Helen interjected, walking between us before we got serious.

"Brody, I kicked your ass back then, and I can kick it now," Booger said, over Helen's raised arm.

"A sucker punch from somebody I thought was family isn't exactly what I call 'kicking my ass,'" I answered between clenched teeth. I could tell Helen was about to take action, so I decided to try and defuse the moment. Offering my hand, I calmly said, "Fred, that was long ago, and far away. We need to work together and be a little professional. Peace?"

Freddie didn't extend a hand. "Just stay in your lane, Brody, and try not to get in the way of a professional."

I resisted an urge to punch his lights out then and there, then remembered my father's long friendship with Helen, and resisted.

7
Done Diver

A month later, after working eleven "dry" holes, we anchored over Helen's twelfth spot on her spreadsheet. After magging the approximate location, she settled over a promising ferrous metal signature. "It's about a hundred feet below us, gentlemen. No snorkeling today." She pointed to the tanks secured to one side of the deck, at the green-striped ones. Noting the Nitrox they held, she announced, "Gear up! You can do thirty minutes on the bottom at that depth without a decompression stop. For this dive, let's call that the maximum time below."

I nodded my head, understanding her instructions. I had already known the time allowable on Nitrox at a hundred feet, without a stop or two to let the nitrogen bubbles come out of my bloodstream. Many years ago, my dad nearly died from the bends. He had to surface from a deep dive off the coast of England without the equipment for decompression. I had no appetite to experience the same.

It was a refreshing change to go scuba diving today. After diving at eleven other sites with no luck, using only a mask, fins, and snorkel, this was a little more to my liking. Besides, Booger had the breath of a five-year-old and couldn't stay under for more than a minute. He had to bob to the surface constantly. I almost felt like I was solo diving. At least we could work the area a little more thoroughly. I hope.

"You know which end the air comes out of, Booger?" I asked a little sarcastically.

"Just keep out of the way of a real diver, Wahl," Thomas snarled. I knew someday this was gonna come to a confrontation, but it was something to be settled in private, away from Cap.

"It's too deep to blow with the mailboxes, so you're a little on your own," Helen instructed. "For the first dive, just try to see what the magnetometer hit on. If it looks like a real wreck site, you can go back down with detectors." Booger and I sat on the side of the *Hoedown*, made one last check of our gear, and slipped our masks on. Before going in, I turned to Booger and asked, "Hey, do you know why divers always flip backward off the side of a boat?"

"I'm sure I'll get a smart-assed answer, asshole," Booger answered, "But I'll bite. Why?"

"Because," I answered, before biting down on the mouthpiece, "if they flipped forward, they would just end up on the boat deck," and I rolled off into the water.

I've done this literally hundreds of times and it still never gets old. I followed the anchor line down toward the bottom, leisurely kicking, with a little upstream angle to compensate for the current. We were anchored quite a ways from the Gulfstream, but not in it, and I would estimate the current to be no more than one or two knots, a negligible amount, but enough to leave you a half-mile away from your boat if you didn't pay attention.

I got to the bottom and started cruising in a slow pattern, watching the time left on my watch. Instead of a featureless sandy bottom, there was some promising structure, rocks, coral, and lots of fish. Grouper, bottom fish, and even a big cobia were hanging around. Cobia often swim near sharks, and I looked anxiously around but didn't see any predators.

Booger was off on his own, and I really didn't give a rat's ass if he kept to any specific plan. He went out of sight in the twilight within a few minutes. Before fading away, I could see him sweeping sand away for a moment like he saw something, then moving on.

I was nearing the thirty-minute mark when I saw what the mag must have hit on: the tip of an anchor jutting out of the rocks. There was too much encrustation stuck to it to tell if it was recent or really old, and there wasn't enough time to investigate. Seeing nothing more substantial to tie to, I pulled a length of Thinline I had velcroed to my weight belt and tied it to the top of the anchor.

I took my dive knife out of my leg sheath and tapped my tank three times, signaling to Booger that I had found something. He emerged from the gloom in a moment, and I pointed to the anchor, then to my watch indicating our scheduled time on the bottom was up. Expecting an argument, he nodded in agreement and started up the anchor rope toward *Hoedown*.

We handed our tanks and the end of the line up to Cap and climbed aboard. She attached a plastic jug, pulled the line tight, and tossed it over the side. GPS is a wonderful thing, but it could take half an hour to find the wreck again at that depth without a marker. Booger had hardly climbed out of the water when he announced,

"I'm done, Helen. I'm tired of diving dry holes based on your so-called 'secret' locations and wild-assed guesses." He pointed at the distant shoreline. "Take me back, now. I'm heading back to Key West where I can work for a *real* salvage company." That speech surprised me a little. To call a site, especially one that had looked that promising to be dry without a thorough investigation, seemed a little like overkill.

"Booger, nothing would make me happier to see you vanish," I said. He had called the skipper by her name instead of Cap, a title she had well-earned. "I don't see how you can be so fast to jump the gun. After all, there was enough structure down there to merit a better look. And," I pointed out, "it's almost definitely a wreck site, with that anchor. We don't know how old, but I think it's worth some effort."

Cap had listened to Booger's speech and my answer without comment. The mention of an anchor prompted a response. "Anchor?" she said, "What about an anchor?" Then, turning to Booger, she answered with her hands on her hips. "You're welcome to resign from the company, and relinquish any claim to future finds, but as far as going to shore now, the day is young, and the water's calm. You can park your butt until it's time to go home, Fred." I could tell she was close to calling him Booger in response to his calling her Helen.

"No," he answered, standing up. He walked close to Cap, and pointed a finger. "I demand to be taken ashore now! I don't want to stay another minute on this tub, and you can't make me!"

"On second thought," Cap mused, "I can't send Brody down by himself, especially at that depth. I'll pull anchor and head to shore."

Suddenly, I realized why he was calling this a dry hole, why he wanted to leave right now, and why he was still wearing his dive gloves. The water was warm, and we only wore 'shorty' wetsuits but always had gloves on when we dived to protect us from sharp metal, coral, and sharp rocks that were always lurking underwater. I remembered Booger had stopped once and swept away some sand like he'd seen something. In one swift move, I stepped toward him and grabbed his hand, not the one he was pointing at Cap with but the other he was holding close to his chest, and jerked his dive glove off. The unmistakable glint of gold clinked on the deck, as two large coins fell to the floor.

All three of us froze, looking at the doubloons. The reasons he wanted to quit and be taken to the shore were obvious. An eight-escudo gold coin from the 1715 fleet could be worth from twelve to over two hundred thousand dollars.

Booger, never one to do anything brilliant, reacted by trying to throw a haymaker at me that would have taken my head off, had he landed.

But my head wasn't there. I ducked, backed off a step, and like the smart ass that I am, instead of dropping him on the spot, I merely slapped his right cheek. The result was immediate and expected. He moved toward me, wound up, and swung again. This time I hit the left side of his face, open-handed. He swung, I slapped. He swung, I slapped. This went on for a minute. Helen started to move in and break up the fight, realized it wasn't a real fight, and then stood back, amused at Booger's futile swings, and knew that I was in little danger of actually being hit.

"Come on, Brody, fight like a man!" Booger backed up, both fists clenched.

"I don't see any man worth fighting with," I answered calmly, relaxed, my hands at my side. To that answer, he lashed out wildly, lunging at me. I stood to one side and kicked him firmly in the ass when he went by, knocking him off balance and toward the rail. As he tried to catch himself, I put a hand on his back and pushed him over the side. He came up sputtering and started swimming toward the back of the boat and the ladder. I pulled the ladder up and waggled my finger. "No, no!" I said with a laugh. Grabbing a life preserver, I threw it to him. Pointing at the shore, I said, "You wanted to go home; it's that way. I suggest you start now so you can make it back by morning."

Helen touched my arm lightly. Saying it loud enough so that Booger could hear her, she noted with mock concern, "He'd never make it. Between the current and any critters that might be around, he'd either be north of Jacksonville by Sunday or shark shit." She sighed and put the ladder back in the water. "Climb aboard, Booger. You'll get your ride to shore, and I'll make sure by nightfall that every treasure company in Florida knows you are a thief, and," she said with a little giggle, "a lousy fighter."

Thomas crawled up the ladder, his cheeks still red from his bitch slapping. I feinted toward him with my fists up, and he shied away from me as if I was holding a cobra. I relaxed and chuckled. "Sit on that ice chest like a good little boy, and I promise not to slap your pretty little face again." Booger cautiously backed away, glaring, and sat on an ice chest. He never took his eyes off of me and sat quietly for the trip back to shore.

After we hit land and secured the boat, we watched Booger walk away and up the dock. Cap noted with her hands on her hips, "When the fighting started, I was ready to move between you two. That ain't the first fight I've stopped. I knew Bric was an ex-SEAL, but I didn't know you had hand-to-hand fighting skills, too." With a look of admiration, she added. "It looked like a poodle fighting a wolf." She smiled. I looked at her inquiringly. She explained,

"The poodle fights, while the wolf eats."

8
Sebastian Dreaming

After we sent Booger Thomas packing, Helen and I sat down to decide our next steps. She took her clipboard with a blank piece of paper and drew a line down the middle, listing the negatives, or problems, as my father would say, on one side, and the positives and opportunities on the other.

"Now we need to figure out the next steps and determine if this wreck is even right for us to work, or pass it on to an operator with better resources." She took out her pen. "First, let's list the challenges. One. It's too deep to blow. The mailboxes on the *Hoedown* aren't effective below about fifty feet. At a hundred to a hundred and ten, she wouldn't move a piece of lint. Two. At that depth, it's a borderline tech dive. That means you, or any other diver we might bring on, will be sucking Nitrox and undergoing a decompression stop almost every time on the way up."

Helen looked worried. " It will be expensive, time-consuming, and a little dangerous. A lot of your dive-time will be eaten up just getting to the bottom." She brightened. "Now the plus side." Holding the two gold coins in her hand, she smiled, "And thanks to this donation by our ex-comrade, we *know* there's some treasure down there. We just don't know how much."

She pulled out a little jeweler's loop and examined both coins carefully. I sat patiently while she handed each heavy eight escudo coins over to me. My young eyes were a little better, and I could plainly see the dates on each coin.   I had held more than one gold coin in my hands over the years, and my dad had pounded stories about shipwrecked gold into my head since I was ten.

"1702, Mexico mint, clear strike on both sides. It's not a Royal." I found a bunch of Royals off Haiti a few years ago, though I dare not tell Helen the story. "Uh, I have heard about Royals. Aren't they the coins that are carefully prepared for presentation to the King?"

"I've only seen pictures of them. They're beautiful," Helen said, agreeing.

I estimated the value of the coin. "Maybe forty grand." I handed it back and looked closely at the other. "Ah, 1712, from Peru. I would guess worth as much as the other one, maybe a little more."

Helen agreed to both of my estimates and noted, "That wreck is about fourteen miles offshore, in international waters. That means we don't have to share the treasure with Florida or any current salvage license. After we make sure nobody else has arrested the wreck, and I'm sure nobody ever has or I would know, and when we get holy water from the Feds, what we get, we keep." She looked up with a little concern.

"That's all the 'pluses' I can note. There may be more treasure down there; I would even say *probably* there's more down there, but how do we get it? I don't know anyone in these parts that has salvaged at that depth." Looking at me, she asked, "Have you?"

"Personally, I don't, but I bet you, and I know somebody that does." I pulled my phone out of my pocket and punched in a number. The phone rang five times, and I was about to hang up when Dad answered. He was never a slave to automation, and had it been a number he didn't recognize, he would have just let it ring. As always, he didn't exchange pleasantries; he just cut to the chase.

"Hey, Brody, what's up?" I told him about the two eight reals we had in possession, that it was probably from a 1715 wreck and it was lying in over a hundred feet of water, then stopped talking. He didn't need to hear the Booger story. We would share that someday over a rum drink when we both needed a laugh. I heard Bric switch gears and go into what I always called "teacher mode".

"I do know of at least one ship off the coast in deep water that has been successfully salvaged. The *Pulaski*."

Helen nodded in agreement. She obviously had heard about that boat.

"The what?" I asked. I hadn't.

Bric explained, "The steam packet *Pulaski* set off from Savannah, Georgia, with a stop in Charleston and was making its way to Baltimore, carrying some of the wealthiest families in the Southeast. It has often been described as 'the Titanic of its time' given the ship's state-of-the-art design and wealthy patrons.

On June 13, 1838, a boiler exploded, and the boat's midsection was blown to pieces. She sank almost immediately in a hundred and ten feet of water about forty miles off the North Carolina coast. Only two of the steamboat's lifeboats made it to shore. Almost half of the two hundred passengers died. The wreckage of the *Pulaski* wasn't discovered until 2018. Because of the depth, it took several months for divers to find a candlestick holder with the phrase '*SB Pulaski*' engraved on the bottom to confirm it was the *Pulaski*."

"And they were able to salvage her? How?" Helen asked.

Bric ignored her question. He had an attentive audience, and he wasn't about to relinquish it. Yet.

"Divers explored only a fraction of the wreckage, but still found more than five hundred gold and silver coins, along with about ten gold watches. Some of the coins were extremely rare and valuable, dating to the late 1700s."

"But how?" I asked, repeating Cap's question.

I could almost see Dad smile over the phone. "As you know, conventional mailbox blowers can't reach that far down, and the *Pulaski* had lots of overburden. Besides, the wreckage was scattered across three places by the explosion. They located a big boat with large motors and equipped with mailboxes. Some say the engines were a little overkill, but in this case they paid off, and she could blow effectively over 100 feet. There was a little problem," Dad added. "At that depth, even with big blowers, the current will move the effect, so you might have to position the boat up current. It's a complicated project at best."

"This wreck we're working is nearly fourteen miles from shore," Helen mused. "It may be outside any areas under control from treasure companies like Queen's Jewels, and Florida can't even collect their twenty-five percent. It falls under Federal Jurisdiction. We file and 'arrest' the wreck, then we can salvage and keep what we find. But," she said with a furrowed brow, "even with the money the investors have thrown in, anything I might collect from these coins," she stared again at the gold in her hand.

"What few dollars I've banked over the years

wouldn't give me enough to supersize my cheese Whopper. Where would I turn?"

As my father often does, he didn't answer her question directly. Instead, he started ticking off some steps.

"Get a lawyer, file with the government, and 'arrest' the wreck. That could take one or more years. They have to research to make sure nobody else has ever filed a claim. You really can't do a thing until you have that piece of paper."

I could see Cap's shoulders sag a little at the thought of it taking years before she could work the wreck.

"Where will I find, or even afford, a lawyer?" Helen asked.

Ignoring her question, Bric continued, "Not until *then* will you need to find a boat with mailboxes and a buttload of horsepower on each side to move overburden that far down." He hesitated for a moment. "Use sea scooters to get your divers to the bottom in a hurry so you don't waste dive time commuting. Of course, everyone will breathe Nitrox and need to do a decompression stop on the way up to keep from getting the bends." He paused. "I know my son is experienced at that depth. How about the rest of your crew?"

Helen answered faster than I could. "Well, as of this morning, we are down to one diver. Brody." She added, "But I know where I can find a few others, but as you pointed out, I won't need them for a year or two. In the meantime, I need to be able to pay bills, eat, and stuff." I could tell by her furrowed brow that Helen was crunching numbers in her head, and they weren't looking good.

"Leave that part to me," Dad responded, "and a lawyer. Let's say I have a line on resources. I think you've found something worth working on. First things first. File for salvage rights as soon as possible. I'll be in touch."

Before he could hang up, I needed to know more about working a wreck in international waters, legally this time. I was sure Cap might know the law, but I was interested in hearing from experience.

"Bric, what do we know about salvaging a wreck this far offshore?"

Bric took point on this call, although I could tell Helen was well versed in this aspect of treasure hunting. "When it comes to the law of the sea, it's not as quite clear cut as 'finder's keepers,'" he explained. "Whether the treasure is gold and silver coins, or large ingots and bars that are found in a sunken ship, even a crate of goods washed ashore, what's up for grabs depends on where it's found and to whom it belongs."

He added with a chuckle, "The process is more *Law and Order* than *Pirates of the Caribbean*. The question is whether the discovery of goods is deemed salvage or treasure-hunting. Salvage refers to when someone saves property that's lost or abandoned at sea. Under international conventions, the 'salvor' is required to return the found goods to the original owner in return for a reward. Treasure hunting, on the other hand, typically means exploration aimed at unearthing antiquities and other valuables from shipwrecks for financial gain." He paused for a moment to let that sink in. It was more for my benefit than Helen's.

"Treasure hunting is not necessarily salvaging. Salvage is the right to be compensated by the owner where the owner is known and you're in a position to return the property to him. In the case of treasure hunting, like the wreck you are over right now, that's not so, just because the stuff's been lost for so long that no owner can come forward." Bric paused again. "Follow me, Brody?" I nodded, then, remembering he was on speakerphone, said, "Yes." Dad went on. He was teaching me more in ten minutes than I might have learned in two years of college. When it came to treasure hunting, Bric was a human encyclopedia. I think Helen was even picking up a few technical items.

"There are times such deep-sea finds come from companies in the business of trolling the seas for sunken treasures. Like you did with this wreck." He paused for a moment. "Wreck sites are often given a specific name so they can be recognized instead of having to constantly refer to coordinates or just 'that wreck'. Have you named it?"

Cap paused for a moment. "Well, I've never had the opportunity to work a new wreck all by my lonesome," she said slowly. She considered for a few minutes and brightened. "It was the twelfth place we worked this year. Let's name it *Site Twelve*."

"Splendid," Bric answered, "*Site Twelve* it is." He cleared his throat. "Now, back to my little Brody lesson. It's important to claim where the shipwreck is found, and this is a most important point. Whether the find lies within a country's territorial waters is a vital consideration in any treasure hunting case."

I could hear papers rustle again while Dad looked at some notes. "The concept of territorial waters is set out in the United Nations Convention on the Law of the Sea. Most countries have a limit of twelve nautical miles from their coastlines, and if a treasure ship ventures inside that limit to work a site, the company could forfeit its claim to the booty. Usually, in this kind of case, there's a law stating that the treasure belongs to the government. If it's in territorial waters, the Law of the Sea Convention comes in, and the state would decide who owns it and what compensation they are entitled to. In the case of the state of Florida, they get twenty-five percent of what's found, and the pick of those items they deem of significant historical value. It can and often does resort to a court case."

Bric paused again for effect. "A common misconception is that finders can keep their discoveries at sea. But under international law, anyone who finds a wreck must report it. Hiding a shipwreck or its cargo is a federal offense. The 1989 International Convention on Salvage says the salvor, or finder, may be deprived of the whole or part of the payment due if the salvor has been guilty of fraud or other dishonest conduct."

Bric looked at his papers again. I couldn't tell over the phone if he was looking at a looseleaf binder, a book, or a laptop. Either way, he was trying as hard as possible to be accurate.

"The term 'Dishonest Conduct'", he continued, "isn't clearly defined. But if you salvage treasure from a ship outside of territorial waters without consulting the Feds, that definitely counts as fraud, and you could lose everything and a big payday. "If the wreck lies in international waters, and there's no one to claim ownership, the finder is probably in the clear, but you still have to file a claim."

"That sounds complicated, but it's mostly what I already understood," Helen said, shaking her head.

"I'm not sure who to reach out to first."

Bric consulted his notes, but I could tell that other than specific dates, he knew this part of maritime law by heart.

"Assuming that the shipwreck has long been abandoned and that the owners of the shipwreck no longer have any claims to the contents buried in the sea like the wreck you just found, you should first contact the Coast Guard to notify the government of the discovery."

He continued. "In 1987, the United States enacted a law called the Abandoned Shipwreck Act. The law was a response to treasure hunters who found long-lost shipwrecked property. If the shipwreck is found outside of the territorial waters of any state, the general maritime rules concerning the discovery of a shipwreck apply, and the discoverers may be entitled to keep the contents of the shipwreck."

Sounding a bit like 'finders keepers, losers weepers,' he concluded, "The general rule of what you find you keep is one that many underwater discoverers would like to apply, and many times they can. However, all underwater discoverers should take the steps outlined above to make sure that they have the legal right to take title to the property found under the water."

"Sheesh," I mumbled to myself, away from the phone. "Ask him what time it is, and he tells you how to build a watch." Helen dug an elbow into my ribs and motioned me to keep my thoughts to myself.

"I'll be in touch in a few days with the name of a lawyer and who to contact within the government," Bric said. "In the meantime, hang tight."

And without another word, the phone went dead.

Bric was never one for small talk.

I was pretty sure I knew who the "resource" was and why it would take a few days. Bric had to liquidate some investments and arrange for someone to perform a high-definition three-D sonar scan.

Helen sounded a little cautious, "How confident are you that your father can help with this? When he worked for me, he wasn't far from living under a bridge and cooking grunts in a borrowed skillet."

I wanted to ease Cap's mind without letting the cat out of the bag. "Oh, he's gotten past that phase in life. Let's just say he's a little farther from that bridge than when you knew him. If he says he can help, I think you can rest assured he can."

Cap told me she was going to stop her treasure hunting efforts for the season and planned to pull the *Hoedown,* spending the rest of the year refurbishing the boat, doing some maintenance on the diesels, and giving the hull a new coat of gel coat in preparation for working the Site Twelve with fresh equipment.

"There's no sense in burning fuel looking for something else," she explained. "I'll save what our supporters have invested and roll our financial commitments over to next year. In the meantime, I'll plant a garden, maybe write in my diary, and concentrate on securing that wreck."

"Cap, I don't have anything pressing at home. If you don't mind, I'll stick around for a few months and help."

"I've been called a lot of things in my life, but never a fool," she said with a laugh. "Stay as long as you like. I have a spare room. I hope you like baloney sandwiches, and every Sunday I make a hot meal."

I looked at her with curiosity.

"Fried baloney on toast." She laughed again.

I didn't plan to head back home for a month or so, but four days later, I was driving down US 1.

To attend a funeral.

9
Dead

Sunday morning, Helen handed me a copy of the local paper, the *Sebastian Daily,* opened to page four. Without saying a word, she pointed to a headline that read, "Local rental service reports stolen pontoon boat." Mildly interested in why Cap would show me something like that, I read the story, and by the second paragraph, I knew why.

"An eighteen-foot pontoon boat, rented by Sebastian Watercraft Rentals for the day on Sunday, was never returned. The rental company conducted a search of the Intracoastal Waterway, the area to which the small pontoon boat is restricted, without success; at this point, the boat is considered stolen. Fredrick Thomas, 33, of Key West, rented the boat and is currently being sought by Indian River Sheriff's, Sebastian Police, and the Coast Guard. If you have any information, please contact one of these authorities."

I looked up at Helen, knowing now why she showed me the paper. "You don't suppose….?"

I dropped the paper on the table, and we both bolted for the door, nearly jamming ourselves in the doorway when we hit the entrance at the same time. We jumped in Helen's truck, affectionately named "The Beast" for its diesel fuel appetite, and drove to the marina, breaking speed laws all the way and nearly taking out thirty feet of somebody's picket fence. We had planned to pull the Hoedown the day before, but were still looking for a trailer large enough to carry the boat. Idling carefully out of the marina in respect to the manatee population, she got the boat up to plan and headed east as quickly as possible.

At sea level, you can see about three miles to the horizon. I took a pair of binoculars and climbed up the stairs to the bridge. That gave me almost five miles of view. It only took fifteen minutes before I made out the shape of a small boat on the horizon. "I see a boat!" I called down to Cap. "It looks like a pontoon boat. It's right off the bow!"

Looking at her GPS, she confirmed, "It's probably right over the wreck." It was just as we feared. Booger was poaching our wreck. I remembered that he saw us mark the spot with a milk jug.

We idled up to the pontoon and saw a still body in a wetsuit, all curled up and lying on the deck. Two large 100-pound Nitrox tanks, a mask, fins, a BC, and a regulator were strewn about. We tied up to the other boat, and I stepped on board. "Booger?" I said, then knelt next to the motionless figure. With a finger, I felt for his carotid pulse, but the moment I touched him, I already knew what I would find. Turning to Helen, who was still aboard *Hoedown*, I told her, "Radio the Coast Guard. There's no pulse, and the body's cold." With a grim look, I added, "Booger's dead."

We waited for the Coasties to come, and they called in a medical examiner from Vero Beach, who showed up with the cops. They interviewed Cap and me while the medical examiner took tons of pics, and had Booger put in a body bag and loaded on the Coast Guard vessel. "Fred quit three days ago," Helen advised. Not wanting to let anyone know we had found a wreck, she added, "This is near where we were diving when we quit. Apparently, Fred came back to explore on his own. It's not safe for anyone to dive without a partner, especially this deep." She pointed at the deck of the pontoon boat. "That's where we found him, dead. Nobody moved the body." Pointing at me, she added, "Brody touched him to see if there was a pulse, and we called the Coast Guard immediately." The Indian River Sheriff's thanked us, took our address and phone numbers, advised us they would be in touch, and left with a dire, "Don't leave town."

After everyone left and before the rental company came to retrieve their boat, I stepped aboard one last time to look around. I noticed something bright lying in a corner that the medical examiner must have missed, picked it up, and put it in my pocket. We hadn't started working on *Hoedown* yet. What had happened to Booger had us both a little shaken. "I didn't care for him," I said to Helen, "But nobody deserves to die, ever." I shuddered a little. "I've seen too much death in my life already."

The cops got in touch two days later and called us in for another statement. Aside from normal questions, it became obvious they had been talking to other people. "Your other roommate at the rental told us that you and Mr. Thomas didn't get along. He even thought you were close to coming to blows more than once." Looking at his notes, he added, "And you moved out of the rental the day before he went missing, and moved in with Ms. O'Rourke." What can you tell me about your conflict with Mr. Thomas and why did you move in with Ms. O'Rourke?"

"Fred Thomas and I are second cousins," I

answered, understanding how this could look suspicious. *"Should I call my dad? Get a lawyer?* We haven't been friends since we were classmates at Key West High School. It has a little to do with a conflict between my dad's mom's family and his, long before we were born. I know a lot of other Thomases, and we get along just fine."

I realized I was talking fast and trying to defend myself without being charged with anything. *Calm down, Brody, you didn't commit any crime.* "Anyway, he didn't want to dive for Cap, er Ms. O'Rourke anymore, and quit about a week ago." The cops didn't need to know about the stolen coins or Booger getting bitch slapped.

"I guess he went back to where we were diving by himself to the last spot we were before he quit. We saw the story about his taking a pontoon boat and being late returning it, and we decided to investigate the area where we last dived together." I put up my hands and hunched my shoulders, in my most innocent 'aw shucks' attitude. "Who knows why?"

"And why did you move in with Ms. O'Rourke?", the Sheriff asked. "Is there a physical relationship between you two?"

"Gosh, no, officer!", I answered as convincingly as possible, even though the thought had briefly crossed my mind. "She's old! She wants to pull her boat out of the water and do some maintenance. I just volunteered to help a little. That's all. I'm sleeping in the guest room."

I was sure they were grilling Cap in another room. We had already discussed that the two gold coins Booger had tried to steal didn't need to be discussed, and I was pretty sure the rest of our stories would match since we were both telling the truth. Regardless, I was relieved to see her in the lobby when I walked out of the interrogation room. "Nobody went to jail," I noted. "I still wonder what killed Booger."

"That's a mystery that may never be found out," Helen said, a little sadly.

We didn't hear from anyone for two weeks until a Sebastian officer knocked at the door. Looking through the window, I turned to Cap. "Well, she's by herself so I don't think anyone's going to be arrested." She came in, introduced herself, and we all sat around the kitchen table.

Looking at some papers on a clipboard, she didn't waste a lot of time putting us at ease. "Mr. Thomas apparently died of decompression sickness. His tanks were empty, and his dive gauge showed he had been in over a hundred feet of water for almost an hour. From what they could tell, he got aboard with his gear then started to feel the effects of the bends and became incapacitated, but without someone to help him and get him to a bariatric chamber to decompress, he succumbed." She stood up and held out her hand. "It appears Mr. Thomas was the victim of an unfortunate accident and poor judgment."

After the officer left, we sat at the kitchen table in silence. After what seemed like an hour but was more like ten minutes, Cap got up, got on her tiptoes, opened a cupboard, pulled down a green bottle, and took two glasses out of the cupboard. "If there was ever a time to break my own rules, it's today." She showed me the label. "Jameson's," I said with a little admiration. "The favorite of my father's mentor, treasure hunter Bo

Morgan."

"I remember that name when my late husband Henry was still alive," Helen said, almost distantly. "He was a true legend."

10
Conch Funeral

It was only a few days later that the coroner released Booger Thomas' body to his family. I left Cap to attend the funeral. "Stay at home until I call you," Helen advised. "Any work I do on the *Hoedown* is therapeutic, anyway. Give my love to your dad." She looked concerned. "It could be years before we have permission to salvage *Site Twelve*," she reminded me. "Heck, you may be onto something better by then."

I shook my head. "You ain't getting rid of me that fast, Cap. Call when you're ready, and I'll come back up. Dad, er Bric, is committed to helping you get what you need."

In an unexpected gesture, Helen gave me a big hug goodbye. "You've become the son I never had", she said with a little tear coming down her cheek. "Please take care, and I'll see you soon."

The drive down the Keys never gets old, but it was almost mechanical this time. As much as I was looking forward to seeing my dad, the planned drink I hoped to share with the story of Booger's mishaps felt hollow and inappropriate now.

Dad declined my invitation to attend the services. "I don't do funerals," he growled when I asked if he was coming. "Not even my own."

"You should go", I had urged. "There's going to be a lot of relatives I haven't seen for years and more than one that I've never met."

Dad shrugged his shoulders. "Nobody there that I

feel a need to see," he answered.

I asked if he was still feuding with the Thomas family. "Wasn't that nearly a hundred years ago?"

"Just a bunch of rich, stuck-up snobs," he answered with a snort. "No skin off my back if I ever see any of them again. For that matter, with all the run-ins you had with Booger when you were in school, I'm surprised you even went."

It was my turn to shrug my shoulders. "I was one of the first people to find him," I answered. "I felt kinda obligated to be at the funeral. I was coming home anyway."

He couldn't be convinced to come. "Besides, the best pair of shoes I own are those worn-out Sperry Topsiders," he said, pointing at the shoes piled in a corner. "Not exactly funeral appropriate." I looked down at my Reef sandals and shrugged. I doubt I would be kicked out of the services for an unacceptable dress code.

The services were at the old family church, the Methodist Chapel on Fleming. It felt like half the town showed, and the crowd spilled out onto the street. Heck, lots of the Key West natives, especially the old ones, were related to each other. I spent the morning hugging second cousins, great-aunts, uncles, and more than one person I had no earthly idea I was related to.

There was more than one person who asked about Booger's demise, and I answered them with as few words as possible. "Dive accident. Tragic, isn't it? No. I wasn't there when it happened. We both worked for the same salvage company, but it happened on his day off."

Booger's coffin was open, and as I passed by to pay

respects, I leaned over and whispered, "You poor dumb oaf. You killed yourself over a half-ounce of old gold." I reached into my pocket and dropped a small coin between the silk folds of the coffin. "Here," I said softly. "Never say you can't take it with you."

I went back to *Seaglass* after the services. I hadn't taken three steps into the lounge of the yacht when Dad curled up his nose. "You smell like the bottom of my grandma's purse."

"I hugged a lot of old ladies today," I answered.

11
Found Her!

Home. Back on the rock. My birthplace and the only place I really cared to live. Key West is quirky, a little wild, and a lot misunderstood. If it wasn't for our friend Kevin Montclaire and *Hunks* on Duval, we would rarely get west of Searstown or Winn Dixie. Locals don't need downtown. For myself, I would far rather sit waist-deep in water on Marvin Key than on a stool at Sloppy Joe's or Hog's Breath.

It didn't take me long to get back to a routine. We released Mary Beth from her duties the day I got home. She wasn't wearing a ring anymore; I didn't ask what happened to the boy toy and she didn't say. Other than those Marvin Key trips and an occasional snapper and cobia fishing in Florida Bay, Bric was content to stay on the boat most days, doing a little reading and searching on Google for something.

I got back into my morning run routine, taking a full lap around the island every other day. When the days got too hot, I switched to evenings, still avoiding downtown by jogging down quiet tree-lined side streets whenever possible.

I used the cemetery as a landmark, then varied down any of the small streets and alleys, dark and unlit, and nearly devoid of cars. One evening I took Windsor past the Battleship Maine memorial at the cemetery, bent to the west, then turned down Elizabeth to Baker Lane. This was about the darkest, quietest street in Old

Town. More than one house was over a hundred years old and had lain abandoned for decades.

I passed a familiar old mansion, unpainted since World War Two, and probably unoccupied for that long. A shabby blue car, covered in dust, old cardboard boxes, and cobwebs, sat in a falling-down shed. The shed looked weathered enough to have been a carriage barn back when the only mode of transportation on this rock was a horse. At first glance in the gloom, the car looked like it had been there for decades too. Just as I passed the house, with its front door boarded up and windows nearly opaque with grime, I caught a glimmer in one window that looked like candlelight.

Curious.

I chalked it off to a glint from a star, the moon, or a passing aircraft. Nobody would want to live in that hulk. Then my curiosity got the best of me. Abandoned house. Abandoned car. I just had to take a look.

As they say, curiosity killed the cat.

And saved the rat.

The dirt driveway led me to the shed. Using my phone as a flashlight, I saw the car was way too new to be paired with that house. I looked a little closer. "Hmm," I mumbled to myself, "that car looks like it was painted with a mop." I idly scratched at a loose chip in the paint.

Green paint showed underneath.

I jumped back, instinctively grabbed my crotch, spun around, and breathed a little easier when nobody was there.

My heart was pounding out of my chest. Using my

phone's flashlight, I looked more closely at the car. Green Hyundai. I glanced up at the window where I thought I had seen the light. I retreated to the back of the shed and thumbed a saved number.

After four rings, my Uncle John Russell answered. "Brody! Are you back in town?"

It wasn't time for pleasantries. I whispered. "She's here!"

"She? Who?" Then it came to him. "Lilly Albury? Where?"

"I'm on Hudson Lane, off Elizabeth. Ah, third, no fourth house on the left going east."

"On my way," Russell answered. "How do you know? Did you see her?"

I explained the green car crudely painted blue, and the candlelight I saw in a window. "It's got to be her!"

I could hear the car siren over the phone. "I'll call for backup," John said. "Don't be a hero. You know she's capable of killing. I'll be there in five minutes."

I pocketed the phone and stood quietly by a side door for my uncle to arrive. Barely a minute later, a pair of headlights pulled into the driveway. That was fast, I thought. Coming out of the barn, I froze when I didn't see any lights on the car top. Staying in the shadows, I was able to see someone get out of the car with something in his hands. The headlights illuminated a DoorDash bag. Oh boy, a food delivery. Talk about bad timing. The delivery boy set the bag by the side door, knocked on the screen door, and turned to walk away. He hadn't gone three steps when I heard the door creak open, and a small arm reached for the bag.

Like my father, I've never been one to take

instructions from the law, even if it's my uncle. I reached the doorway in three steps and grabbed the arm firmly by the wrist and jerked. I'm glad it was a firm grasp. In two seconds, my hands were full of a kicking, scratching, screaming, eye-gouging, smelly, insane maniac. Barefoot in a filthy nightgown, her voice was a hoarse scream. "KILL ME! KILL ME!", she cried. Before she could do some real damage, I took both hands, spun her around, and took her to the ground as gently as possible.

Confronted with the person who tried to kill me, I wanted nothing to do with retaliating. As calmly as I could, I said, "Take it easy, Lilly. Nobody's going to hurt you. We're going to get you help."

"I DON'T WANT HELP, I WANT TO DIE! KILL ME, YOU BASTARD!"

The DoorDash driver froze halfway to his car. I turned to him and said, "The police will be here in a minute. Pull your car out of the driveway. Let them in and don't leave," I cautioned. "You're a witness, and they will want a report."

It seemed like an hour, but it was only a few minutes later that the street and front yard were smothered in patrol cars and flashing lights. Uncle John was the first to reach me, and instead of taking over, he spoke into the radio clipped to his lapel. "Contact the Mental Health Center and have someone come to our location." He gave the location, then motioned for a female officer to take over, and I stood up. Uncle John took me by the arm and led me to his patrol car. "I'm taking you to the medical center. No sense waiting for an ambulance."

I pulled away from him. "I don't need a hospital. A

ride home would be fine." Uncle John shook his head.
"What's that, ketchup on your cheek?
Your face looks like you went three rounds with a
bobcat," he answered, "and I would just guess those
nails weren't exactly hospital-grade sanitary." I put my
hand to my face, and blood came away. I nodded
silently, got in the squad car, and rode to Lower Keys
Medical Center in silence, deep in thought. Uncle John
took me to the E.R. and waited until I was released.

"Nothing deep enough for stitches," the nurse said
kindly. "What happened? Grabbed your pet cat
wrong?" It was Hilda, the woman who helped patch me
up. I thought for a second and didn't see a need to
elaborate. "Something like that," was my answer.
Hilda didn't ask any more questions, which was fine
with me, and didn't comment on the Monroe Sheriff
who stayed with me. She just cleaned the scratches,
applied antibiotic ointment to the spots, and got a
prescription from the doc. She understood I was deep
in thought and in no mood to chat.

I heard from Uncle John a few days later. The
house was a disastrous mess. No power, no water, no
working bathroom. She had been holed up there since
the night she tried to whack me, ordering food on a
throw-away cell phone, and paying for it using
CashApp, replenishing it at a local convenience store
late at night. The entire downstairs of the house was
piled knee-deep with used food containers, feces, and
old food delivery bags. "They took her off the Keys,
where she's being treated for her mental illness," Uncle
John related. "I have no idea if or when she will ever
be able to return to society."

12
Big Secret

Life returned to normal aboard the *Seaglass*, if there's such a thing as normal on this rock. Bric stayed at home for the most part, and I ventured downtown every few nights to have a drink or three at *Hunks*. I never got rid of my houseboat, and without going into lurid details, let's just say I didn't go back to the boat every night and usually fared better than my father's criteria used to be - any girl with more teeth than tattoos.

Enough said.

I taught Mary Beth to snorkel, and we spent many Saturday afternoons on her day off from the bank, exploring places far from the tourist crowds near San Key light. She was, as my dad would say, easy on the eyes, and wore swimsuits that would make a Sports Illustrated model blush. With her red mane flowing in the water, all she needed were tailfins instead of flippers, and she would have been the perfect image of *The Little Mermaid*.

Let's just say I could find less attractive people to swim with.

I kept up my diving, going out with some of my and my dad's buddies, and occasionally touched base with Helen for any news. It took a year and a half, but one day she called.

"We've got it!" she exclaimed. "*Site Twelve* is ours!"

"I'll pack right now. I can be there by dark!" was

my excited answer.

"First things first," she cautioned. "Is your dad nearby? Can you put him on speaker?"

I propped the phone up on the table between Bric and me. His answer almost surprised me. "I've been expecting your call," he growled. "I've been talking to people, and I've got two boats ready to join the effort, and have sufficient funding to support them. Are you ready on your end? I'm thinking three other divers, besides Brody."

"They will be here in a week," she answered. "Veteran divers, all qualified on Nitrox and experienced with deep dives. I'll make arrangements for shoreside accommodations." Pausing momentarily, she collected her thoughts regarding fuel. "With diesel costs like they are now, motoring ten miles out and back every day is going to run up a heck of a bill. Plus, the time spent coming and going to the site will restrict our dive time unless we leave the marina before light and return after dark."

Ignoring her concerns like he often does, Bric pointed out, "I think before you do anything, you should get that detailed three-D image of the surroundings. That will tell you where to zero in on. Otherwise, you could blow a hundred square feet and miss what you're looking for by ten. I have some people that will head your way today. You and Brody can lead them to the site when they get there. I'll have some other details soon. Don't worry about housing either. I have a solution for that." He smiled again. "I can tell you see money flying out the window. Don't concern yourself. I've got it all covered." As always, he hung up without saying goodbye. After making sure the phone was shut off, he looked at me with serious eyes.

"I don't need to tell you my involvement is just between us and a fencepost. I have secured the services of the perfect ship, over a hundred and thirty feet long, with twin German-made MAN diesels, both pumping out just a little over a thousand horsepower each. What's best, it already has mailboxes installed." I could see the twinkle in Bric's eyes as I suddenly realized what ship he was talking about. "*Never on Saturday*! The Cohen's yacht! Have you talked to David? Where's she at?"

"Slow down, hold your horses, buckaroo," Bric cautioned. "One question at a time. Yes, I talked to David last week. He's in Barcelona pursuing another doctorate in some obscure language, but at the mention that there might be a previously undocumented galleon, he said he would drop everything, take a sabbatical, and be here when needed."

"And the *Saturday*?" I asked, still excited.

"All buttoned up safely at a marina in Port Everglades. He said he would locate Hop Sing, and have him get her provisioned, fueled, and loaded for bear when we have the green light."

"A thousand horsepower per side," I mused. "Have they ever blown with both engines at full throttle?"

"There's never been an opportunity for *Saturday* to salvage a wreck this deep," Bric answered. "Normally, according to David, her diesels blow at about twenty-five percent of throttle. That will clear overburden at thirty-five to fifty feet." Dad looked at some notes. "The mailboxes were designed specifically for her, so they're confident they can take full throttle, but in normal cases, it would be like driving an Indy car to the Wal-Mart, and blow anything of value underneath her into another zip code."

Changing gears, Bric lapsed back into pure business mode. "When you get down there, have Helen send me her bank info, and I'll have a few hundred grand deposited. She'll have cash on hand to buy more equipment if needed."

I nodded, understanding. "Anything else before I head out?"

"Just let Helen know I'll be in touch regarding the terms for this investment and that I will be the facilitator of this part of the project."

"OK, Dad. Should I send David instructions on how to find us, or will you?"

"I'll do a little better than that," he answered, "I'll be on her."

Before I got up to pack, I thought of something else. "You mentioned accommodations."

His answer was a little roundabout. "I'm as concerned as Helen is about the distance from shore and fuel costs. It could eat well into any profit, IF there is any, so I called an old buddy and got a long-term loan on the only boat short of a small cruise ship."

"And what ship is that?" I asked.

You'll find out in a week," he answered, grinning. "Let's just say it's a big secret."

13
Home Away From Home

A week later, I was on the dive site with Helen when I saw the familiar white superstructure of the *Never on Saturday* loom into view, my father standing on the flying bridge at the bow, looking like a senior-citizen version of Leonardo De Caprio in *Titanic*.

He dropped anchor, and we came aboard, and I went aboard to meet David. After introductions, we all gathered around a twenty-four-inch monitor while

David played the three-D sonar scan that had been conducted a few days earlier. I was pleased to get a full view of the site after groping around in the gloom for twenty minutes. David knew as much about this kind of sonar reading as the people who did the scan, and he conducted the meeting like a professor teaching a class.

Pointing at the screen, he noted, "You can see several guns lying several yards away on both sides of what appears to be the wreck." Squinting at the screen, he calculated, "I would guess at least ten meters or more. That's a little strange."

He pointed at another form. "There's the anchor, almost fifty meters away." He looked at how the *Saturday* was sitting at anchor and returned his gaze to the screen. "With the main part of the wreck in one place and assuming the Gulfstream was running in the same direction it is today, which I know it was, I would guess when she went down she was already at anchor. I don't see any debris field north or south of the wreck, so," pointing at the heavily overgrown wreck, "I would hazard a guess that if you are going to find anything, it will probably be there."

David pulled out some ruler-looking stick with a moving guide attached to it.

"What's that?" I asked.

Bric answered before David could, looking slightly annoyed that I even asked.

"Brody, that's a slide rule. The home computer, before there was such a thing."

Absently, David nodded without looking up. "A Slipstick doesn't need electricity, and it's twice as fast as opening an Excel spreadsheet, especially when you are just looking for a quick and dirty answer." Holding the ruler up, he added, "This is my go-to way to calculate. Grandpa Cohen taught me how to use it when I was about ten, and it always stuck with me."

Having explained more than I expected him to, he went back to his calculations.

"Let's see, figuring a one-knot current, a hundred feet of depth, the Saturday running at full thrust…" his voice trailed off as he made some calculations. Looking up with a smile, he declared, "I estimate we anchor fifty-two feet upstream from the wreck and blow at full throttle for thirty minutes. The upside is that the current, what little there is, should move the silt away from the wreck fairly fast."

"Well, what are we waiting for?" I asked. "Time's a wastin'."

David, in his all-business demeanor, answered with a definitive, "I concur." With respect, he turned to Cap, who had so far stood in the background, recognizing a technology that went far beyond her experience. "Captain, it's your call," he said.

Helen shook her head. "This is all going faster than I imagined. The rest of the crew won't be here for a few more days." Looking around the *Never On Saturday,* she added, "Bric, you said you had an angle on accommodations and saving fuel. I assume you plan to host everyone on this beautiful, er, yacht. Is that your plan?"

"*Never on* Saturday could accommodate everybody on this operation, with a little inventive bedding," Bric answered with a smile. "But I think *Big Secret* is a better option."

"So, what's the big secret?" Helen asked.

"It's not what, it's who," Dad answered with a laugh. "*Big Secret* is a boat. A boat as you've never seen." Bric looked at his phone for the time. "May I use your radio, Cap?"

With a little shrug, she pointed at the unit. "Help yourself."

Adjusting the frequency, he keyed the mic. "*Big Secret, Big Secret*, copy Bric Wahl?"

"Roger, Captain Bric, Jamal here", came a voice with an Island twang. "What's your location, mon?"

Reluctant to give an exact location over the air, Dad told them to go due east of the Sebastian inlet and look for a big white yacht. "Roger, mon, see you in an hour." About an hour and a half later, the strangest ship I'd ever seen lumbered into view. Before she arrived, Bric held a hand toward the boat.

"Behold *Big Secret*, thirty years old, ninety-six feet long, twenty-four wide. Built as a liveaboard salvage vessel in shallow waters, she has five staterooms with double berths, an owner's stateroom," nodding toward Helen, "Two baths, a washer and dryer, a full galley, provisions for a month on the water, 2400 gallons of potable water, and a thousand gallons per day fresh water maker. She's got air conditioning, two generators, seven thousand gallons of fuel, a dive compressor, and an eight-ton capacity crane that's capable of dragging up anything on the bottom smaller than an airplane." Chuckling, he added. "I've been told she's sailed under more than one name and has a very checkered past. Let's just say if you vacuum up the main deck, you could shoot it, snort it, or inject it, no doubt with interesting effects." With a bow, he concluded, "I give you Hotel *Big Secret*."

Helen stood there, almost speechless. With wonder, she nearly whispered, "We can stay out here for two weeks or more at a time, easy. I've never seen something like this, not to mention even heard of one."

Bric pointed at the main cabin of the *Saturday*. "David and I will stay aboard this boat." He smiled when he added, "We'll manage." Nodding toward me, he said, "Brody, you've got run of the dive crew quarters in the bow."

I shook my head. "No, Dad, I'll stay with the crew aboard the *Secret*. I ain't no better than the rest of the gang. I'll be just fine there."

It took a few weeks to get the other divers aboard comfortable with their surroundings and familiar with what they were going to dive on. We all made some quick and dirty dives with less than thirty minutes on the bottom, so we didn't need a decompression stop on the way back up, and got comfortable with the sea scooters.

Finally, it was time to get serious. Using Nitrox, two of us went to the bottom and, using radios, tweaked *Saturday's* mailbox thrust until it was blowing over what appeared to be the main part of the wreck.

As soon as the silt cleared, both of us swarmed on the cleared spot like kids converging on a broken *piñata* and eagerly started looking for huge piles of gold coins. Other than a few promising encrusted lumps that were too big to carry to the surface, nothing was clearly visible.

At the end of our hour, we slowly paddled to our halfway decompression spot, changed tanks, and waited for another agonizing hour. We got to the surface, eager to don fresh tanks and head back down, but Cap held her hands up. "Wait," she said firmly. "Stick to the plan." Pointing to Ben and Ralph, she instructed, "Team two! Suit up!"

"But Cap!" I answered, groaning, "I'm not tired. Two hours underwater isn't even a breather for me." I looked at my father for support. He looked away, seeming engrossed in the shape of a passing cloud. Bric knew who the *real* boss was.

14
Cobs

They call it *working* a wreck, because that's what it is – work, especially when you're salvaging a ship that sank in a hundred feet of water. It adds multi-dimensions to a tedious project. We could only work at the bottom for an hour at a time, and even with sea scooters to get us to the wreck in a hurry, it seemed like mere minutes before you had to start your decompression routine on the way back to the surface.

All four divers were in excellent health, and Cap eventually agreed to let us each do three dives a day, with an hour rest while the other team went down. Hop Sing, the chef on Never on Saturday, assumed double duty, cooking breakfast and dinner for the dive crew aboard the Big Secret and returning to the yacht to cook meals for David and Dad.

After a grueling day in the water, the dive crew, including yours truly, wasn't picky at dinner time. I think you could have shoveled coal into us and we wouldn't have complained.

After *Saturday* blew the site up two more times, we got serious about looking for treasure. Despite Booger's finding three gold escudos, we didn't find many gold coins. After two weeks, there wasn't more than a small handful of coins. We *did* find lots of ferrous metal, guns, iron nails, and spikes. *Big Secret* had rows of plastic tubs on the deck, all equipped with solutions and low-voltage electrodes, that slowly dissolved encrustation on the artifacts. It was evident that the wreck had undergone some sort of cataclysmic event. "Many of the metal items are twisted and bent, like they were in some sort of explosion," David observed, "which is consistent with there not being a real debris field."

After a week, Dad asked to be taken to shore. "It looks like you guys have it all under control. I miss my own bed and, er, I have some things to attend to." Looking at me, he asked, "Brody, can I borrow your beater Jeep to get home?"

I went below and brought up my keys. "So," I said, a little sarcastically, "it's good enough to drive home?"

"I have half a mind to catch a ride to Vero Beach and buy a *real* car," he answered, just as sarcastically, "but I guess for a four-hour drive, I'll struggle by."

"Wait", I asked. "Do I need to call Mary Beth to give you your nightly shot?"

He answered with his usual growl. "I can manage. Oh, if she wants to come by occasionally and tell me she loves her daddy, let her know it's okay with me."

"I wouldn't hold my breath," I answered. "She's warmed from pure hatred with you to 'tolerable', but you'd better leave well enough alone."

Dad merely answered me with another low growl, like a cornered wolf.

We settled into a routine, a little dull and tedious. Oh, we dug and probed and looked for gold, but it was apparent this wasn't a huge galleon with vast amounts of gold.

But there was silver. Lots of silver.

We expected to find either big lumps of coins, pieces of eight that had been in chests long since rotted away, or bulky silver bars weighing as much as seventy pounds. But on my second dive down, I radioed to Cap to have *Big Secret* lower a rope from her crane, because I had something that looked heavy. They looked like nothing less than a stack of breadsticks, only smaller in diameter, and they were in a lump, easily more than fifty pounds. One other detail excited me.

They were non-ferrous.

When we brought the first lump up, David and Helen were both examining it by the time I was done with my decompression stop, cleaning the encrustation off one end, and scratching the surface with a thick-bladed knife.

"Is it silver?" I asked. "I'm pretty sure it's silver, but I've never seen anything like it."

"I've only read about them," David admitted, slowly. "I'm pretty sure it's a lump of silver ingots for making cobs."

"Cobs?" Helen and I both said at the same time. We knew the term. David, the ever-present professor, explained anyway. "Molten silver was poured out on a stone slab and carefully molded into bars, then each bar was cut into chunks or planchets of the appropriate weight. These small silver clumps were struck with a hammer between crude dies. In fact, the Spanish word 'cabo' is the source of the English 'cob' and means 'the end'. In this instance, the clump of silver was clipped off the end of the bar. The size, shape, and impression of these cobs were often irregular, but they were always the proper weight. Many cobs were quite thick and disfigured with large cracks."

Helen nodded her head in understanding, but had a question. "So, why do you think the uncut silver bars were on this wreck?"

It was David's turn to shake his head. "Your guess

is as good as mine," he said. "Perhaps they didn't have time before sailing to turn them into coins. After all, once they returned to Spain, most silver coins were re-melted and turned into jewelry, more refined silver coins, and other items. Or," he said with a smile, "they might have been undocumented cargo. I would hazard all of the ships in the 1715 fleet, and every other galleon that sailed for Spain had as much unregistered treasure as what was on the ships' manifest. It was a common practice."

"How much are they worth?" Helen asked. David rubbed his day-old beard and thought for a moment. He answered carefully. "Coins from the 1715 fleet, any coin, is worth at least twelve hundred, up to as much as two grand if it's in really good shape and has a visible date. Normally, bulk silver from these ships is more likely to be melted down and turned into replica coins." He looked at his phone for reference. "In a bezel, maybe one-fifty to two hundred."

Cap sounded disappointed. "So valuable but no home run."

"I wouldn't be so sure," David answered. "Uncut bars like these are rare. I doubt more than a few dozen have ever been found on any wreck. Cleaned and preserved, I would bet that just about every serious collector would love one of these among their possessions."

"I don't think there are that many collectors in the world," I said slowly. "I counted a few dozen of those lumps down there, and that was just at a glance."

As it turned out, *Big Secret* was a godsend. I'm not saying we couldn't have brought all that silver up without her crane, but it made it a helluva lot easier.

We thought there was more down there, but we had to pull up all those pesky lumps of silver first. *Big Secret* brought them up, and each was placed in a tub with the solution and slowly restored to its shiny new look. The bars were rugged and uneven, looking like so many breadsticks at an Italian restaurant.

The crew went to shore to celebrate every two weeks and went mildly wild for two days, then dragged ass back to the *Hoedown* on Monday mornings for the return trip to the site. Helen didn't approve of the gang over-imbibing and partaking in general debauchery, but understood that boys will be boys, even if they are in their late twenties and early thirties. To avoid sending hungover divers down, she restricted Mondays to non-dive days, while everyone cleaned their findings, cataloged, and sorted.

15
Gut Punch

I had lost track of time, and nearly six weeks had gone by without speaking to my father. We usually touched base at least once a week, and I felt a pang of guilt when I saw on my cell that he'd called.

At ten miles out, cell phone service was, at best, spotty and, at worst, non-existent. I borrowed David's satphone and gave him a buzz.

"Hey, Dad, what's up? All's good on this end. We're bringing more silver up every day." I was excited, chattering without giving him a chance to answer.

"Hey, Brody," came a soft answer. Bric sounded tired.

"You okay?" I asked, concerned, "You don't sound good."

"I'm fine," he responded. "I've got a little favor to ask you."

"Sure, Dad, anything," was all I thought to say.

"These nightly shots are becoming a pain in the ass, literally. I wonder if you could convince your sister to drop by and stick with me every afternoon? She doesn't have to stay, just drop by. Anyway," he admitted, "I miss her."

Coming from someone who never asked for anything, this was almost earth-shaking. "Sure, Pop. Let me get Mary Beth on the line, and I'll conference you back in on a three-way call." Helen overheard my side of the call and asked, "Is everything okay?"

"I'm not sure," I answered. "Bric never asks for much, and he wants me to talk my sister into visiting once a day." I went on to explain the cordial but strained relationship with his illegitimate daughter. Helen shook her head in understanding. "I have family that doesn't speak to me very often," she admitted without adding details. I got Mary Beth on the phone after she got off work, and told her that Dad wanted to talk to both of us.

"Frankly, I'm a little weary of sticking needles in his hairy ass," she said. I could almost see her tossing her red hair like she does when she's angry. I didn't answer, so after a few moments, she caved a little. "Oh, go ahead, put him on the line. I'm not a fan of this, but I need to hear him beg a little."

Without another word, I added Dad into the call. "Hi, Mary Beth. Still love me?" It was a sarcastic question and got a sarcastic answer. "Like life itself, Bric," she said, almost spitting the words out. The line was silent for a moment. Then Dad spoke again, softly this time.

"I would like you to start coming by again for this darn diabetes shot if you could. You don't have to stay unless you want to, just come by every afternoon for a few minutes." He sounded even more tired.

"Every day?" she asked. "I have a life, Bric. Maybe a few times a week, but every day? I don't think so. Give me one good reason why I should suddenly start coming around and do something you have been doing just fine by yourself for months."

After hearing every sarcastic "Brickisim" line possible over the years, his answer was the last one I ever expected. After a moment's silence, he answered.

"Because I'm dying."

The phone went silent. I didn't even know if we were still connected for a moment. Mary was quiet, and I couldn't think of anything to say. Bric finally broke the silence.

Two words said it all. "Pancreatic cancer", Bric said grimly. "Stage three, or worse, inoperable, almost untreatable, nearly always terminal."

My dad was a man of few words.

"You said 'almost'", I pointed out, shaking at the thought of losing my father. "What can be done? Radiation, Chemo?"

"Maybe both," he answered. "I've been going to the Lower Keys Cancer Center for treatments for over a month. I suspect I might get a little sick before I get a lot sick. Chemo tries to kill cancer before the chemo kills you. Sometimes it does, sometimes it doesn't."

My next question was the elephant in the room, the question I hated to ask but needed to.

"How long?"

"Six months or so if I don't do anything and if the treatment helps, maybe two years." He chuckled a little. "At first, I said 'fuck it', I've been there, done that, got the shirt, so to speak. But now," Bric said, "I think I'll let the doctors see what they can do so I can do a few more turns around that ol' sun."

"How do you feel?" I asked, cautiously, wanting to change the subject, more than anything. Before he could answer, I added, "By the way, I'm heading home. Now."

"Nonsense!" he almost growled. "If I don't need someone to help me barf down a toilet by now, it's no time to start. Let's just say I have extensive experience in that skill. You stay there. It's an opportunity of a lifetime for you to work on a previously undiscovered wreck, especially a 1715 wreck. I'll be just fine here."

I dug in my heels. I got my stubborn streak from one of the best- the man I was talking to.

"I still don't think this is the best summer to spend away…." My voice trailed off, not knowing how to broach an awkward subject.

Helen, hearing both ends of the call on the speakerphone, whispered. "Go home and be with your father. I'll take you to Vero Beach, where you can rent a car."

"That's right," I whispered back, with my hand over the cellphone. "I forgot the Jeep is already in Key West." With my hand off the phone, I said, "Mary Beth, no need to come to the boat. I'll be home in five hours."

"I'd still like you to come and stay for a while, Mary Beth," Bric said to my sister. "Well, daughter, are you willing to bury the hatchet for a month or so and take care of your old man? And I don't mean bury the hatchet in my back one night when I'm asleep."

Mary answered almost in a whisper. "Yes, Bric. I'll move onto *Seaglass* and be there as long as you need, or until…."

I could hear her start to softly cry over the phone. I think Dad's news knocked a chink out of her armor.

I used my father's trick and hung up without another word, never giving him a chance to argue. David, overhearing the conversation, said, "Hand me the phone. I'll have a float plane come here and pick you up." He took the phone and turned away to make a call. Helen, used to a frugal lifestyle where spare pocket change made the difference between a Big Mac and Top Ramen, raised her eyebrows at how casually David ordered a pricey charter to Key West.

It was nearly dusk when a Cessna 406 floatplane circled *Seaglass* and settled softly onto the calm ocean. Helen and I took *Big Secret's* little Zodiac out to meet the idling plane. Hugging me before I boarded, Helen softly said, "Brody, stay as long as you want, or need to. I promise you will receive your full share of the treasure, and Bric will receive his percentage. I wouldn't have even tried to work the *Site Twelve* without his help."

I stepped into the cockpit of the Cessna and was surprised to see a familiar face. "Billy!" Mr. Goodman's private pilot gave me a warm handshake. "Sorry it took so long, but it took a while to find this baby." He patted the wheel as if it were a pet. "With what they charged me, I almost called David to see if I could buy her. She's one sweet ride."

As we lifted off, I looked out the window one last time at our little flotilla of treasure boats. The *Site Twelve* project would have to go on without me for now and the foreseeable future. My father was far more important to me than some old silver.

We landed in Key West just after dark. Billy chose to use the landing gear on the 406 instead of her floats and parked at the executive terminal, where I could catch a cab. I reached for Billy's hand to thank him, and he pushed it away to give me a big hug.

"Go take care of your father," he said with a soft voice. "My prayers are with him." I didn't trust my voice to answer and just nodded my head, fighting back tears.

When I got to *Seaglass,* it was dark. Mary Beth was there and gave me a big hug. Dad got up and reached out to shake my hand. I ignored his hand and gave him a big hug, too. I never saw my father with much hair, but now, hatless, he was as bald as a cueball.

As she promised, Mary Beth moved back onto the yacht, and we settled down to a regular if slightly dysfunctional routine. Dad kept his twice-monthly visits to the cancer center, and the days varied between chipper and upbeat to not being able to stray far from a toilet. He was getting thinner and a little more tired each time. The chemo was kicking his ass, but he wouldn't admit it.

After six treatments, he was given a reprieve to see if there was much response. He started perking up almost immediately, and Mary took a little break, heading off-island for a little getaway. Bric kept his regular visits with the oncologist, but wouldn't share any updates with me, so I had to call him myself.

The phrase "no news is good news" is not always true.

16
Green Flash

A few months later, out of the blue, Bric asked, "Son, I'm between treatments and feeling half-assed human for the first time in months. You up for a little sail?"

"Sure!" I answered without hesitation. "San Juan, Cartagena, Nassau?"

Bric held up two hands, "Slow down, buckaroo, just an afternoon sunset cruise in the Gulf was what I had in mind."

Dad was through his latest regimen of chemotherapy and radiation. I looked at my father. He was down to 140 pounds, but a few weeks after his last treatment, he was starting to get a little color back in his cheeks, and his step seemed a little lighter. "I haven't seen a decent sundown in months," he said with a faraway look. "I don't want to watch cats jump through hoops, or have some jerk put a parrot on my shoulder. Just you, me, and a real Keys sunset is all I crave." With a questioning look, he added, "Up to it?"

"Always, Pops, you know that. *Mary Beth* can be ready to go in five minutes."

It almost broke my heart, but we got rid of the *Seaglass* and moved back into my houseboat. The yacht, a 155-foot motorsailer, was traded for a fifty-five-foot sloop plus a buttload of cash. We never asked where the money came from that bought the *Seaglass,* and didn't think it appropriate to ask where the money came from when we traded it. I'm sure I didn't get the best deal for the *Seaglass*, but Dad was living on my houseboat now, and the yacht was just wasting away in the harbor.

I looked around until I found Cookie a good position on another yacht, cooking dinners for people with more money than brains. He scored a good gig, and even though there were a few tears on both sides when we parted, we both knew it was the best way to end a valued relationship. Cookie had become almost a member of the family. We promised to stay in touch, and both of us knew we probably wouldn't.

I eased *Mary Beth* out of the harbor under power and raised the sails as soon as we left the channel between Key West and Sunset Key. The breeze was gentle, and we literally sailed toward the sunset, veering away from the numerous sunset booze cruises that left the island every afternoon. Once clear and distant from any other boats, I dropped the sails, and we quietly drifted with nothing but a gentle lapping of waves on the hull and an occasional blow from a family of accompanying dolphins. I mixed a boat drink for both of us, and we watched the sun dip to the horizon.

"The sky is perfect for one of my favorite moments," Dad said after sipping his drink.

"What's that?" I asked

"That rarest of rare phenomena," Bric said, with a twinge of sadness. I knew better than to interrupt his explanation. After almost a minute, he finished his thought.

"The green flash," he said. "It's been years since I've seen one. Not that there haven't been hundreds, just that I didn't take the time to look." Pointing at the horizon with a shaking finger as the sun touched the water, he said, almost in a whisper, "There! Any second now. Watch!"

The green flash is a phenomenon that occurs at sunset when conditions are just right and results from two optical phenomena combining: a mirage and the dispersion of sunlight. As the sun dips below the horizon, the light is dispersed through the Earth's atmosphere like a prism, and there's a brief, almost instant flash of chartreuse on the horizon.

I peered at the orange ball as it slowly sank into the water. Just as it went out of sight, I waited for that magic moment, but as the sun did, despite the supposed perfect conditions, there was no green flash.

"Ah, well", Bric said with a sigh. "You just never know. I was hoping tonight, one last time…."

"Last time, Dad?" I asked. "We can come out here every night until we see one. I'm done diving for the year. We can see lots of green flashes. Dozens."

Dad stood up from his chair and set his drink on a table. "That we can do, son, that we can do." Folding his arms, he turned to me. "Do you mind taking *Mary Beth* back to the harbor on your own? With the sun going down, it's getting a little chilly. I think I'll go below deck and take a little sport nap. We can go to *Hunks* for a nightcap with Kevin before we head back to the houseboat." Moving toward the stairs, he said over his shoulder, "Give me a hand down the stairs, son. They're steep and my knees ain't what they used to be."

"Sure, Dad, no problem."

Epilogue

The *Mary Beth* bobbed gently at anchor in the afternoon breeze, a hundred yards or more west of Boca Grande Key. Comfortably sitting in thirty feet of crystal-clear water, I could see little reef fish darting through the eelgrass with a few Queen Conchs lumbering along, minding their own business. I sat by myself, sipping a mojito, and spied the shore where it all began a dozen or so years ago. I peered at the low rise.

The shallow holes where Karen and Bric found those gold bars way back when had long been obliterated by wind, rain, and waves during the many storms that had passed through since then. My father had been explicit about his wishes after he was gone. There were to be no services of any kind, no mourning and no crying, just a big party, and a true celebration of life. Most importantly, there would never be a service in a church He didn't make, but rather over an ocean He did. And if I didn't do his bidding, he would meet me in heaven for a thorough ass-kicking.

Yeah, like *he's* gonna be there.

After topping off my drink, I climbed into the little rubber Zodiac and motored my way to shore, carrying my beverage in one hand and precious cargo wedged firmly between my bare feet. Sliding up to shore, I stepped out, surveyed the landscape and that one lone palm tree that's been there for years, curving into the wind. "Well, Pop, I guess this is as good a place as any." Bric had told me about his onetime lover and sometime girlfriend, Rio Rio, who once said that he couldn't die, that Superman never dies. Dad did indeed dodge more than one bullet through the years. I smiled to myself a little.

If he were a cat, he would have been about four lives in the hole.

I lifted the lid off the urn. Stepping into the water until the ripples lapped at my calves, I poured the ashes into the clear water, then pulled the lid off my drink and poured it onto the growing ring of ash. "Here's to you, old man." I didn't have a prepared speech and just said whatever came to mind. "To the best father a kid could ever have. You fought the good fight. I can only wish I have half the adventures you did. Sail on, Bric Wahl."

I stepped back into the Zodiac just as the sun slipped below the horizon into the gulf. If I had blinked, I would have missed it, but the most brilliant green flash graced the sunset, a vision beyond spectacular.

With a chuckle, I said out loud, "There you go, Dad, you finally got your green flash. Happy?"

I made the boat ride back to Key West alone, just as it was going out, but strangely, it seemed just a little lonelier. There would be a gathering at Hunks that night, as he requested. It was to be a celebration, a party with free-flowing alcohol in his honor. No doubt people would get drunk, people would get laid, and everyone would go home happy tonight.

He wouldn't want it any other way.

As dusk turned to darkness, I took my Costas off and pointed the *Mary Beth* into a brisk, quartering breeze and unfurled all of her sails. The wind in my face was strong enough to bring tears to my eyes.

Yeah. Sure. It was the wind.

Author's Notes

I originally thought this would be my last book in the Bric Whal series. There are only so many ways you can stab, shoot, kidnap, and otherwise create mayhem for one individual. It's hard for a series, whether it be novel, TV, or movie, to get much past three seasons, series, or episodes. The main character almost always turns dark when a writer runs out of fresh ideas. I'm rather pleased that I managed to drag Bric through nine, but I thought that all things, even good things, must come to an end.

Not yet.

Writing is like a drug habit. As soon as you publish the "last" book, your mind starts conjuring up new adventures. I guess I'll keep doing it until I go blind.

Hopefully that's not next week.

Like all of the Bric Wahl series, even though this book can stand alone, if you haven't read the previous eight, some subtleties may escape you. This isn't a shameless ploy to get you to buy all the books; it's just that starting with *Once Upon a Time in Key West* will make you feel like you are walking into the latest Star Wars movie in the middle of the film without ever having seen the others; lots of action, but a plot that you will never understand.

People to recognize. Of course, we'll start with my treasure hunting buddy Bill Black, Owner/Operator of Search and Salvage. He's on the water every summer looking for remnants of the fleet that wrecked off the East Coast of Florida in 1715. Many of the ships were found and stripped of their fabulous wealth in gold and silver, and many remain undiscovered.

There are an estimated half-billion dollars in treasure out there, and he's out to find it. Part of this book is based on that search, which is why it's called treasure hunting rather than treasure finding. His stories, his introductions to his friends and co-workers, and his comments on my drafts have made this and many of my other books more believable and accurate. Believe me, contrary to adventure TV shows, you don't walk down a beach after a storm and pick up pocketsful of gold and silver coins.

Thanks again to Mark 'Caretaker' Strussenberg for reviewing some of this book before going to print.

As always, a special nod to my loving wife, Tina. I apologize to you in advance for writing something I tried to do four books ago. Tina and Karen Thurman (*The real Karen*) thought I was crazy at the time

They may be right; I may be crazy.

You will find out what that something is later in the book.

Also, a special shout-out to my friend Ellen O'Neal. Ellen is the singer and leader of the Phoenix Band, a local group that plays contemporary and classic rock at various restaurants, bars, and parties on the central east coast of Florida. We first heard Phoenix when they played at our community, Lamplighter Village.

I mentioned to Ellen once that I had recently purchased a bass guitar (my third childhood; I have quit and sold my gear twice before over the past forty years). She invited me to sit in for a few songs one night, and I have played with the band several times since. Over the past two years, Ellen and the band have become close friends with Tina and me. She's the inspiration for my new character, Helen.

Thank you, Peter Leonard, for taking over the editing duties. I ain't the easiest person to edit. Peter and I have been friends for as long as I've been writing books.

Peter is a New York City native with a degree in journalism from Brockport State University, NY. After moving to South Florida in 1987, he began selling airtime for various radio stations and writing and producing many memorable commercials. Peter has worked in air and on camera and is a stickler for detail. His hobbies include comedy writing and performing, and playing keyboards for anyone who'll have him.

I've been a guest on a number of his radio shows, including several appearances on THE FOOD FOR THOUGHT RADIO SHOW, where I had the opportunity to put on my chef's hat and talk about the many cooking competitions I have competed in and won. Peter's been doing FM shows for eighteen years and now hosts an internet show on WEINETWORK.

This is his first collaboration with me, and I think his work has raised the bar a few feet. He makes even *me* sound good.

Be careful what you wish for.

Enjoy, and thank you to my readers for your kind words, loyalty, support, and patience.

**Also Available on Amazon By Wayne Gales
in Kindle, Paperback and Audible**

Treasure Key
Key West Camouflage
Nobody's Inn Key West
Everybody's Bar in Key West
Southernmost Exposure
Southernmost Son
Bone Island Bodies
Once Upon a Time in Key West
Living and Dying in Key West Time
All three available on Audible as a Trilogy
Texas in the Tropics
What Happens in Key West
Under The Rock
All three available on Audible as a Trilogy

No Guilt – Healthy Dishes
and Family Favorite Recipes

Children's books, illustrated by Lori Kus

We Wish to Fish
Sun, Sand, and the Salty Sea
Caught No Fish

Children's books, illustrated by Ariel Torres

Ari and the Pirate
Daniella Digs a Dino

About the Author

Imagine a life lived to the fullest, a journey that has taken you from the thrill of professional motorcycle racing to the depths of the ocean in pursuit of long-lost treasure. A life where you've traveled the world, won awards for your culinary creations, and unearthed a rich family history that spans over a century. This is the remarkable life of Wayne Gales, an author, chef, and marketer who has lived a story worthy of his own novels.

Born with a taste for adventure, Wayne's wanderlust led him to visit all fifty states and twenty-three countries, immersing himself in diverse cultures and experiences. But it was his time spent in the Florida Keys that truly shaped his story. Living on a houseboat and closely following the narrative of the novel Treasure Key, Wayne found himself in the heart of the treasure hunting scene, befriending local legends like Robert Moran, former Vice President of Marketing for Treasure Salvors, Inc. - the company responsible for discovering the legendary Atocha treasure.

These real-life encounters sparked Wayne's imagination and fueled his desire to write. Drawing on his experiences and the characters he met, Wayne began crafting the Bric Wahl series, a collection of eleven novels featuring a tough, soldier-of-fortune protagonist inspired by his own adventures.

Now settled in Melbourne, Florida, with his wife Tina, Wayne continues to write, bringing his vibrant story to life on the page. His work is a testament to the power of pursuing one's passions and the incredible journeys that can result from a life lived with courage and curiosity

www.ingramcontent.com/pod-product-compliance
Lightning Source LLC
Chambersburg PA
CBHW012015110726
47993CB00009B/3070